VICTORIAN WORKHOUSE

My Story.

VICTORIAN
WORKHOUSE

The Diary of
Edith Lorrimer, England 1871

By Pamela Oldfield

While the events described and some of the characters in this book
may be based on actual historical events and real people, Edith Lorrimer is a
fictional character, created by the author, and her diary is a work of fiction.

Scholastic Children's Books
Commonwealth House, 1–19 New Oxford Street,
London, WC1A 1NU, UK
A division of Scholastic Ltd
London ~ New York ~ Toronto ~ Sydney ~ Auckland
Mexico City ~ New Delhi ~ Hong Kong

Published in the UK by Scholastic Ltd, 2004

Text copyright © Pamela Oldfield, 2004

ISBN 0 439 97730 4

All rights reserved
Printed by AIT Nørhaven A/S, Denmark
Cover image supplied by Bridgeman Art Library
Background image supplied by Hulton Archive

2 4 6 8 10 9 7 5 3 1

The right of Pamela Oldfield to be identified as the author of
this work has been asserted by her in accordance with the
Copyright, Designs and Patents Act, 1988.

Stoneleigh, Kent, 1871

Thursday 19th January, 1871

What a terrible, never-to-be-forgotten day – my first ever visit to the workhouse. I have come early to bed with a headache and it is all thanks to Mama and a girl named Rosie Chubb (a cosy name for such a wild creature!). Mama was determined that today I should attend a meeting at Stoneleigh Workhouse. She insists that helping the poor is a charitable duty, but for her it is different. She has a passion for waifs and strays and for the past year has been a member of the Board of Guardians at the workhouse.

I am Edith Lorrimer, aged fifteen (sixteen next month) and, inspired by Florence Nightingale's example, hope I might train to be a nurse, but Mama says it is hardly suitable work for a respectable young woman.

She summed it up briskly. "Long hours, Edith, hard work, suffering, death and grief!"

Instead she suggested that I learn something of the work she undertakes and I reluctantly agreed. Now that I have met Rosie Chubb, I *can* understand Mama's interest in it. But to start at the beginning…

Stoneleigh Workhouse is a dreadful place. "Hellish" may be a better word. I confess I was deeply shocked. From the outside it is a grim-looking building with rows of uncurtained windows, and the way in is through a large oak door that creaks and groans like a banshee when it swings open on its huge hinges.

My spirits plummeted further the moment I stepped inside. To my way of thinking it is more like a prison than a place where destitute people are saved from ruin. It was bleak in the extreme and the occasional hissing gaslights did little to dispel the gloom. High, echoing corridors, dark green paint and not a single ornament or decoration to lighten the depressing effect. The smell of stale food was terrible (stewed boots, I shouldn't wonder), plus there was a strong hint of old clothes, sickness and damp. One breath of it and my insides curdled. I complained to Mama but she told me not to fuss.

"The residents have to live with the smell," she said. "It will do you no harm."

It is January but there seemed to be little in the way of heating, though somewhere there must have been a fire because ghostly wisps of bitter-smelling smoke drifted in the cold air of the gloomy corridor. An old woman approached us on shuffling feet, head bent, hands clasped as though in prayer. As she drew nearer

I saw that her lips moved in silent speech and her gaze was fixed on the ground. A frayed sacking apron covered her skirt. She wore no bonnet and her grey hair straggled like rats' tails. I tried to find a word of greeting but my throat was dry and none came. Mama smiled. "Good morning, Mrs Lynch." The old woman walked straight past as though we didn't exist. Mama said, "Poor soul. She's very deaf."

Suddenly I came to an abrupt halt. "I can hear sobbing," I whispered. "From somewhere upstairs." We listened and heard a woman's voice raised in anger. Then a man's voice. "Lucy! Lucy!"

I glanced at Mama, who laid her hand on my arm. We then heard a loud slap followed by a scream and Mama's fingers tightened. A door slammed and footsteps clattered along the corridor above our heads. I felt afraid for no good reason, the hair on the back of my neck stood up and I was grateful for Mama's company. The sobbing was resumed and then a furious thumping began, as though someone was beating their fists against a door. Mama sighed heavily.

"What shall we do?" I whispered.

"Nothing, Edith. Discipline is an internal matter." She spoke firmly, yet I felt her anxiety was as strong as my own.

We waited for the meeting in a dingy office full of files and ledgers. There was a rug on the floor and a comfortable chair for the workhouse Master. His name is Alfred Frumley and I took against him instantly. He is big and burly with a flat nose and dark, gimlet eyes. His mouth has a cruel twist to it and he gives the impression that he doesn't know what love means. Why, I wondered, was he appointed to such a position? Does he rule with an iron will? If he had power over me I would tremble.

Mama protests that I exaggerate, but the truth is she doesn't like him either because he calls the workhouse people "inmates". She likes to call them residents because inmates makes them sound like prisoners.

"Isn't that exactly what they are?" I argued rashly. "These people are there because they are feckless."

"Feckless?" Mama gave me one of her "looks". "Of course they are feckless, but you make that sound like a crime. Feckless means being inadequate for some reason – being weak in body or mind. Being puny or blind. Quite unemployable, in fact. They are born with these problems, or acquire them, and cannot rise above them."

"I'm sorry, Mama, I—"

"They are not to blame, Edith, and they deserve our compassion. They are not in the workhouse as a punishment. Rather, they are offered sanctuary because they have nowhere else to go."

"But how do they get out?"

"Some never do. The authorities have a duty to care for such unfortunates and they have built the workhouses to guarantee them food and shelter."

I could find no answer and stayed silent.

She went on more calmly. "Remember, Edith, we must never allow them to give up hope. They must be encouraged to retain their dignity."

Papa used to say that Mama is beautiful when she is angry and I suddenly saw what he meant. Colour had come into her cheeks and her eyes flashed. Poor Mama. Papa died seven years ago and she still misses him most dreadfully, yet things are not as bad as they might be. We have ample money and to spare. We live in a charming, rambling house fronting the street on the outskirts of Stoneleigh, with Theo, my "adopted cousin". We have the luxury of two live-in servants – Cook, who comes originally from Ireland, and Amy, a maid. We also have a part-time gardener. The house has four bedrooms and Cook and Amy live in the attic rooms above. We also have a yard for hanging out the washing and a small garden. Mama's dream is to live in a house that has a garden lawn large enough to allow a game of croquet. Mine is to learn archery. It is such an elegant sport for a woman and everyone who is anyone in Stoneleigh has taken it up.

Stoneleigh is ten miles from Canterbury and is surrounded by farms and woods. Kent is famous for its cherries, hops and apples. Local people, gipsies and hundreds of families that come down here from the east of London pick the hops in September. (The hops are used to make beer.) Amy comes from the east of London and before she became our maid she used to pick hops every September with her mother and brothers. That way they earned enough money to buy coal for their winter fires.

Farmers bring their animals to Stoneleigh Market on the far side of town on Mondays and then the streets are loud with the mooing of cattle, the baa-ing of sheep and the grunts and squeals of assorted pigs.

When Amy brought up my night-time glass of hot milk I asked her how she would like to end up in a workhouse, and she shuddered.

"Lordsakes, Miss Edith! What a terrible thought! I'd die of shame and misery." She told me about her great-aunt Matilda, a cheerful spinster. She worked as a milliner but when her sight failed she could no longer work and, with no income, was forced to enter the workhouse.

"And she never spoke another word," Amy told me, wide-eyed. "She was dumb until the day she died! Wouldn't see any visitors. Wouldn't speak. Wouldn't eat. She *willed* herself to die!" Amy said that someone should tell Queen Victoria about the workhouses and the poor souls who end up in them.

"Surely her ministers have told her already," I protested.

"Maybe they don't dare to," said Amy.

I have just had a splendid idea. Tomorrow, in this diary, I shall begin my story about Rosie Chubb – a child of the workhouse – since she has no education and cannot write her own diary. What a sad, fascinating creature she is.

Friday 20th January

Am now sitting at the table with my diary, watching through the window for the first snowflakes to fall. John, the gardener, says it won't be long now. He thinks he can foretell the weather from a piece of seaweed he found on the beach at Margate years ago.

Prince, my dearest spaniel, is snoring beside me. He is very old and deaf and needs a lot of care. As for supporting himself – he couldn't catch a rabbit to save his life! But he potters about happily, knowing how much he is loved. He has a better life than any of those sad people in the workhouse.

Last night I dreamed I was walking along that gloomy workhouse corridor, and it was very dark and full of echoes, and Rosie Chubb was calling to me for help from the other end. I tried to run towards her but my legs were so heavy, I knew I could never reach the end of the corridor. I saw a candle in the distance and in its flickering light I saw Rosie with a cat perched on her shoulder, but instead of being green, the cat's eyes were red and glowing. Suddenly Rosie began to glide towards me, but as I called her name she reached out to touch me – and at once turned into the old woman we had passed in the corridor. Then, before my horrified eyes, she and the cat began to crumble and became nothing more than a heap of dust upon the flagstones…

I woke screaming and sat up as the church clock was striking midnight. I was trembling all over and do hope it was not a bad omen.

Now I dip my pen into the inkwell with a heartfelt sigh as I prepare to tell of my first sight of Rosie Chubb. At yesterday's Board Meeting she was dragged into the room by Mrs Noye, who is on the staff there. Rosie was struggling wildly and Mrs Noye was shouting at her, but suddenly Rosie bit the woman's hand and made her escape. We could hear her laughing as she clattered down the corridor in her awful, ill-fitting boots. Five minutes later, a little more subdued, she was brought back again and I took a good look at her.

I think she is about my age, perhaps a little older, with untidy red hair. Mama sees a certain wild beauty in the girl but her careless looks do not impress me. I suppose her eyes are her best feature – green, with long pale lashes. The workhouse uniform is a shapeless brown garment, which scarcely reaches her scrawny ankles. A regulation shawl made of striped blanket was wrapped around her shoulders and her ugly bonnet was askew. I saw her glance at my new jacket with the fur trim and at my new, very elegant, buttoned boots.

"What has she done now?" asked Mama.

Mrs Noye nursed her bitten hand and glared at the girl. "Feeding that stray cat again. As if we haven't got enough mouths to feed."

Rosie stuck out her tongue and was given a resounding slap across the face.

"Don't strike her!" cried Mama. "If she fed the poor creature it was a kindness. Surely we must applaud her for that."

Rosie rounded on her. "What do you care? You rich people make me sick!"

For this ungrateful remark she received another slap from Mrs Noye and a good shaking. I would have been reeling from the blows but Rosie tossed her head, totally defiant. It was amazing how little she cared about the power they had over her. I was truly impressed.

"That cat should be put down," Mrs Noye insisted. "It's a horrible mangy creature with only one ear."

Rosie gave a short laugh. "'E's a sight more 'andsome than you, and you've got two ears!"

I laughed – I couldn't help it – and Rosie caught my eye and winked. It made me feel strangely like an ally, but everyone else on the Board turned to glare at me and Mama hissed, "*Edith*!" and gave me one of her withering looks. I at once apologized to Mrs Noye and dared not look at Rosie.

Rosie said, "They were scraps from me own plate I give the cat. It was *my* food."

Frumley snorted. "Stolen from the kitchen, more likely." He regarded her with obvious dislike. "But since you insist it was your own food, Chubb, we are obviously giving you too much to eat. You shall go on restricted rations for a week." He nodded to Mrs Noye who looked pleased at the punishment.

Rosie gave a scornful laugh. "Restricted rations? If you give me nothing at all I should 'ardly notice the difference!" She glanced at me, grinning.

Frumley reddened angrily. "Then for the first day you shall have nothing at all. See if you notice that, you impudent girl!"

Appalled I cried out, "That's much too harsh!"

He turned his gimlet eyes on me. "Please do not interfere, Miss Lorrimer. You are not a member of the Board of Guardians, remember, and are here on sufferance only because your mother requested it."

Rosie was dragged out again but not before she had shouted a few curses, which I will not write down. A fishwife might learn some new words from Rosie Chubb, I thought!

As we walked home, I asked Mama what rations they were given. It seems that the women have four ounces of cooked meat a day with a few potatoes, thin porridge and gruel. And ten ounces of bread per day to go with the gruel. It sounds revolting but Mama says they are grateful for it and funds do not allow for more. Tomorrow Rosie Chubb will have nothing to eat. Today I am looking forward to a midday meal of baked salmon and gratin potatoes. Tonight it will be cold meat and a slice of quince tart. I almost feel guilty.

I asked Mama why they could not be given more food but she said that they must not have more than the countless people who do *not* enter the workhouse, but somehow scrape a meagre living and manage to survive. Those people resent the money the government is spending on the workhouse inmates – money which they rightly claim comes from hard-working people's taxes.

"So what will become of Rosie Chubb?" I asked. "Can't they find her some employment?"

It seems that they have found her several jobs, but she is her own worst enemy. She lies and steals and upsets the rest of the staff until the employers return her to the workhouse as "entirely unsuitable". In her place I would do anything to change my environment.

I asked why the workhouses are such wretched places.

"Some people feel that if they are too comfortable it will encourage people to do less for themselves and they might pretend to be destitute." Mama ended by saying, "Thank the Lord we women do not have the vote, Edith. Nor should I care to be a Member of Parliament and have to make these very difficult decisions. If the destitute are left to die in the streets it is labelled 'scandalous' but if money is spent on workhouses to help them, everyone grumbles about the expense."

Saturday 21st January

A letter from Cousin Theo at last. He is not my real cousin but was adopted by Mama's friend Katherine many years ago, for reasons I do not quite understand. When Katherine died Theo came to live with us. He was only seven then and is more like an older brother than a cousin to me. He is in Spain now and coming home soon. But for how long? Theo has what Mama calls "wanderlust" and has always wanted to travel extensively. He had wanted to go to Paris, but hostilities continue between France and Prussia and make a visit impossible. There is also some trouble in Italy. In fact it seems that much of Europe is in a state of deep unrest at present.

But to get back to Theo… When he does return, our house will echo once again with his practice sessions at the piano. He does play well and so he should, for he started to play at the age of five, poor boy. Yet he seems to enjoy it. I have truly missed him but shall not tell him so, for he is already much too vain.

The Reverend John Bursell paid us a visit this morning and sent Cook into a flurry because she had too few biscuits to offer. Instead she hastily made a tray of currant scones (knowing the vicar's appetite), which he greatly enjoyed. He was collecting contributions for the Church Fund in order to take the children of his Sunday School on their annual summer picnic in July. This is held in the grounds of the squire's house. Plenty of bread, butter and jam is served, followed by fat slices of carraway cake and gallons of lemon barley water. The children look forward to it all year.

Sunday 22nd January

Arrived at church five minutes late (which mortified Mama) and tiptoed into our family pew. A dozen or so poor people from the town sat on the free seats at the back, while others stood in a huddle wearing their Sunday best. They were all holding hymn books, though I suspect few of them can read. Many of the men will have left school early, probably when they were no older than ten, and found work in the fields. The girls will have gone into service to help eke out the father's pitiful income. Their clothes may be hand-me-downs and their survival a constant struggle against debt, unemployment or sickness, yet they are all proud to be living independently and look down on those reduced to living in the workhouse.

The sermon was "Love thy neighbour" and Mama nudged me. I knew at once she was reminding me that one day she would like me to replace her on the Board of Guardians. That can only happen after her death when I inherit the property, and I do not want to think about being without her.

I knelt and put my hands together and prayed most earnestly – for Mama and Theo, for Cook and Amy, and for my darling Prince, who is not well. He seems restless and has no appetite. I begged God to restore him to health. I cannot imagine life without my faithful old dog. I also prayed for Rosie that she might mend her ways and somehow find a useful life outside the workhouse. I hope God was listening.

Monday 23rd January

Great excitement. Theo arrived home just after lunch and brought me a piece of lace as a gift. Bless the boy! He is now even more of a dandy than he was before. Twenty years old and with a sweet girlish face. He

22

most resembles a choirboy! His fair curly hair is now longer than ever, his shoes the very height of fashion and he has affected a short stick which he tucks under his arm like a sergeant major. I have told him how foolish he looks (someone needs to take him down a peg!) and have hidden the stick under my bed.

Almost his first question was about his hero, Dr Livingstone (our famous explorer who disappeared in Africa four years ago). Mama told him that an expedition has been set up to look for him led by an American journalist called Henry Stanley. We shall have to pray that they are successful. Theo already has plans to go abroad again, maybe next year. He wants to see the newly opened Suez Canal, among other things. It certainly is one of the wonders of the world.

Theo has had a most stimulating time. I am quite envious. He can go where and when he pleases but I remain at home. Hopefully, when I am older, Mama and I will travel together to Rome, where she has a distant cousin.

I keep thinking about poor Rosie Chubb on her restricted rations. And that pathetic one-eared cat of hers. Perhaps by now someone has put the poor thing out of its misery. If only Rosie could have her hair trimmed she might look halfway personable. (I hate the way Frumley calls her Chubb.) I wish my hair curled like Rosie's. Mine is dark brown and straight as a die and requires dozens of curling rags before it looks anything. Life is so unfair.

Thursday 26th January

Snow fell during the night. We awoke to find two inches at least and Stoneleigh transformed by its whiteness. Poor Prince was most displeased. He hates the cold and has not recovered his spirits.

Another meeting at the workhouse. Fresh snow was falling as Mama hurried me along but although I grumbled I was secretly not *too* reluctant. I wanted to see Rosie again.

To my surprise, Frumley smiled at me when I arrived – if you can call it a smile. (It more closely resembled a leer.)

"My dear Miss Lorrimer," said the slimy wretch. "What a pleasure to see you again."

I could not return the compliment so forced a thin

smile and said nothing. He reminds me of a shapeless slug. I found myself wondering if he helps himself to the food that he holds back from those he punishes. A spiteful idea, but why not? Who is to stop him? I asked Mama but she was shocked and said he would not dare. He would lose his job. But only if he is found out, I told her.

There are many Board members but two of them are Mother's especial friends. Leonard Price, who is tall, thin and elderly, and who once ran his own private school for rich boys. Also Mrs Pleshey, who is a nervous sparrow of a woman and always fiddling with the fringe of a beautiful silk shawl (she has several). The poor soul was jilted at the altar years ago and is now about 45, with money left her by an aunt. If I wished to join the Board of Guardians I should have to wait for a vacancy and then offer my services to the workhouse Master and hope to be elected from a number of applicants. These members are mostly wealthy people who can afford to give both time and money. People who give to charity are well respected in Stoneleigh.

The agenda for the Board Meeting dragged on. It seems there are repairs to the roof, which are becoming urgent, but for which the workhouse does not have sufficient funds. Mr Frumley wants the work done by a friend of his "in the trade" who will do it cheaply, but Leonard Price has asked for three estimates, which did not please Frumley at all. I wonder if he was planning to pocket the difference. Oh dear! How wicked of me. What a terribly suspicious mind I have! I won't mention *that* unkind thought to Mama.

Then some excitement. A woman arrived at the workhouse door asking for indoor relief and was ushered into the meeting and offered a seat. Mama explained later that "indoor relief" means the woman is taken *into* the workhouse – in other words, becomes an *in*mate. Indoors. (The alternative is "outdoor" relief. This is financial help given to someone who does not need to become an inmate but is *temporarily* in need. A man who has been ill might owe a week's rent and if he is reimbursed for the amount, he can remain outside the workhouse, return to work and regain his independence.)

The woman's name is Fanny Barker. Tearfully, in a weak voice, she explained that she is a married woman whose husband has recently deserted her. She is suffering from advanced consumption, has no money and claimed she hadn't eaten for two days. I could easily believe her. Gaunt as a skeleton and with a dreadful cough that seemed to shake her whole body, she was almost too weak to brush the snow from her coat. Despite the shame of her situation she was throwing herself on our mercy. Frumley, the brute, was all for sending her away.

"You say you were born in Canterbury, Mrs Barker," he said. "Why don't you apply to Canterbury for relief? That's where you originated and by rights the expense should be borne by them."

Fanny Barker looked frightened at the prospect of a further long walk through the snow. She tried to speak, but tears of weakness filled her eyes and she began to cry.

"She will never reach the next town," Mama protested. "Look at her. She is at the end of her tether! She needs a doctor. Do you have a spare bed in the infirmary?"

Frumley pretended not to know, Mrs Noye fussed with her pen and the members of the Board exchanged exasperated glances.

Suddenly the poor woman staggered to her feet. "If you send me away from here, I shall lie down and die on your doorstep!" she cried. "I swear to God I cannot walk another step." She was stopped by a bout of coughing. "I'm a respectable woman. Do you imagine I would choose to come cap in hand like a beggar? You, Mr Frumley, are a heartless brute!" She collapsed back on to the chair and Frumley had the grace to look embarrassed by the sad outburst.

Mrs Noye said hastily that there were two spare beds, but Frumley still would not agree. It seems the workhouses have a certain amount of money allotted each year, which can be increased in cases of emergency. He obviously tries to spend as meagrely as he can, presumably in the hope that his superiors will be impressed by his thrift. Stupid, selfish beast. I wanted to shake him until his eyes popped out.

Leonard Price glared at the workhouse Master. "It would be cruel to turn Mrs Barker away from Stoneleigh. The walk to Canterbury in this weather will kill her – and if she carries out her threat and *dies* on our doorstep, that will look very bad!"

Faced with this unpalatable truth, Frumley gave in with bad grace and there were sighs of relief all round.

It's clear that Fanny Barker will need a doctor urgently. I am haunted by her expression when she saw her name entered in the workhouse ledger in Mrs Noye's spidery handwriting. Horror at her terrible predicament, but relief that she would have a roof over her head and something to eat.

When the meeting ended I was taken on a tour of the premises, and a more miserable place would be hard to find. We went into the bathhouse, where poor Fanny Barker was taking a bath under the supercilious eye of Mrs Noye. The bathhouse was a freezing cold place with dark tiles on the walls and a stone flagged floor. It was lit by a single gas bracket high up on the wall. I saw four baths and a row of basins on a long wooden trestle. Mrs Barker was shivering as she knelt in a few inches of cold water while she tried to wash her hair with a bar of soap which would not lather. Mrs Noye was holding a worn towel on which Fanny Barker would eventually dry herself.

I was told that her own clothes had been taken away and would be thoroughly steamed in a special machine to kill any lice. To replace her clothes she would be given the workhouse uniform. The poor soul was obviously embarrassed and I left immediately. How dreadful to be naked and watched by curious strangers. So much for Mama and her hopes of dignity for the unfortunates incarcerated here, I thought sadly.

Apparently Fanny Barker had brought with her a small loom on which she once wove articles to sell, but this was immediately confiscated and will be sold to help pay for her keep. According to Mama, if an applicant has anything of value they cannot be declared destitute and therefore cannot be taken into the workhouse. They first have to prove that they are without the wherewithal to buy themselves food and shelter.

"So Mrs Barker will never again be able to earn any money," I said, astonished.

Mama shrugged. "It is a foolish law," she admitted, "but we have to abide by it."

I was shown the laundry – a vast noisy sunless room full of steam and the sharp smell of soapsuds. I counted seven women slaving over the large tubs where the clothes are washed, their reddened faces shiny with sweat. Some kind of bleach or disinfectant is obviously used and the smell made my eyes sting. Condensation ran down the windows and pooled on the floor. Heavy wooden racks are pulled up and down from the high ceiling and the sheets and clothes are draped over them and hoisted up to the ceiling from where they drip on to the unfortunates toiling beneath. No doubt Rosie takes her turn in here. Just thinking of it filled my eyes with tears. What a terrible existence. I could imagine Rosie waking each morning with nothing to look forward to except drudgery, poor food and the less than stimulating company of the other inmates. (Do they ever gossip or laugh among themselves? Are they allowed to?) Not forgetting the punishments. Is Rosie the only rebel? Is she the only person in Stoneleigh Workhouse with a spark of resentment for the cards she has been dealt and the courage to fight back against every injustice? If so, she must be very lonely. I was told I could see the dining room and dormitories at a later date. Of Rosie herself there was no sign and when I enquired no one wanted to disclose her whereabouts, which I think is a bad sign. Is she in more trouble?

I went home feeling depressed, but Theo challenged me to a snowball fight and we ran about, hurling snow at each other, screaming like children, until finally my cheerful spirits returned.

Wednesday 1st February

Another week has passed. The snow has now turned to a horrid brown slush and my buttoned boots are quite ruined from it. I shall have to have a new pair. I found myself wondering about Rosie's boots and then, lo and behold! Just after two o'clock, when Mama was absent from the house on an errand, Rosie knocked at our door. I stared at her in disbelief, delighted to see her again. She had a grubby cloth bundle tucked under her arm.

"What on earth are you doing here?" I asked, astonished. "Are you allowed to wander about in the town?"

"No." She rolled her eyes. "I've just slipped out to—"

I was at once alarmed for her. "Rosie! Suppose they find out?"

"Then I'll be punished. Brought you this." She pointed to the bundle. Something inside it was wriggling about. "It's me cat. I thought you could do something useful for a change and take care of 'im."

Without thinking I said, "Mama doesn't like cats."

The cat, an elderly tabby, had managed to get his head free and now stared around suspiciously. He looked really odd, with his one ear and a frightened expression on his face.

"'E'll be safe with you, Edie. You've got a kind face."

"My name's Edith," I told her. "Not Edie." Mama hates me to be called Edie. She says it makes me sound like a servant.

Rosie went on. "'E'll still be my cat but you'll be taking care of 'im for me."

"No!" I stared at her aghast. "I'm sorry, Rosie, but we have Prince, my dog. They wouldn't get along."

"Right then. I'll wring the cat's neck here and now, for that's what Frumley'll do if he catches 'im." She gave me a challenging look. "I'd rather do it than let old Frumley get 'is dirty hands on the poor creature." Setting actions to words she dragged the cat from the cloth bag and closed her poor roughened hands around its neck. The cat began to wriggle and scratch, and my heart began to race.

Horrified, I cried, "Rosie! Don't!"

We looked at each other. Would she really do it? She looked crazy enough. I knew I was beaten. "Very well then," I muttered, with a bad grace.

Rosie released the animal and rolled up the old bag. She turned to go, then paused. "'Is favourite food is jellied eels. I pinched some from Frumley's supper once and Oddsey went mad for 'em."

"Oddsey?"

"That's 'is name."

She turned to go, but I put out a hand to restrain her. "Rosie..." I began hesitantly. "Forgive me for asking, but where were you last Thursday? I came to the workhouse, but couldn't see you anywhere."

She put her head on one side, thinking back. "I was shut in the coal cellar all day for complaining about the bread they gave us for breakfast. It was stale with mould. Disgusting! I refused to eat it and threw it on the floor. Old Frumley nearly had a fit. He picked it up and tried to make me eat it, but I spat it out all down the front of his waistcoat!" She laughed at the memory, but then her face darkened. "Mind you, it was dark down there. And quiet. Just me and the rat."

Appalled, I stared at her, seeing the scene in my mind. A rat! I shuddered.

She went on. "There was nothing to do except muck about with the coal and coke so I mixed a lot of it up. Sat on it, kicked it around, threw some at the rat… Not a lot you can do with coal."

"Was it very dark?"

"My eyes got used to it. There were one or two chinks in the brickwork and a sort of grating 'igh up." She gave me a crooked smile. "When Mrs Noye let me out I said, 'Thanks. That was a lot of fun!'" Her voice hardened. "They'll never get the better of me!"

We looked at each other for a long time. Then I said, "Rosie, do you ever pray?"

"To 'im, you mean?" She jerked a disrespectful thumb at the sky.

I nodded. "You could ask him to save you from the workhouse. To offer you a way out. I pray for you each night before I go to bed."

"Do you really?" She gave me an odd look. "I've tried it," she told me with a toss of her head. "I've asked

34

him over and over but he never listens. He doesn't have time for the likes of us!"

Before I could protest, she had gone, running erratically down the road with her arms outstretched, waving them up and down like a giant bird so that people stared at her and shook their heads. I sighed. Another chapter in Rosie's unhappy story.

I glanced down at Oddsey who was sitting on the front step washing himself, while his tail flicked angrily. I knew how he felt! I groaned. Mangy was the only way to describe him, but perhaps with a bath and some proper food...

I bent to stroke him. "If Rosie loves you, I love you," I told him, and went into the kitchen to find a saucer and some milk.

Thursday 2nd February

Morning. Tripped over a basket of oranges, which had been left inside the front door. My left shin is badly grazed but I received little sympathy from

Mama. It seems the fruit is intended for the residents at the workhouse. Mama has discovered that they never have fresh fruit and is determined to change that. A nice surprise for Rosie, I thought.

Evening ... eight o'clock

We went to the workhouse again this afternoon. The doctor had been called to an elderly woman by the name of Mona Cripps who is near to death. Frumley insisted they had no money for doctors so Mama agreed to pay the bill.

Mama also told the Board about the weekly oranges. I wonder if the inmates will ever see them or if Frumley will spirit them away. Probably his wife will turn them into marmalade for her husband's breakfast toast. Mama is too trusting by far.

While I was there I visited the dining room, which consisted of a couple of dozen benches set alongside bare trestle tables. A middle-aged woman was laying cutlery – or should I say a motley assortment of spoons that have seen better days. (At least the food isn't eaten with bare hands as happens in some workhouses, where they also have to "drink" the thin porridge straight from the bowls.) The smell of stale food was most unpleasant, despite the existence of two large windows. These are covered with whitewash so the sky is not visible and the room is made darker than it need be. I doubt if the windows are ever opened. The walls are bare except for two large boards. One bears the legend "GOD IS TRUTH" and the other "GOD IS GOOD". I tried to imagine Rosie sitting among the others, scooping gruel into her mouth with a rusty spoon.

On one of the tables I saw a pair of brass scales and was told that since legislation in 1834 it is standard practice, so that any inmate may ask to have his rations weighed. This is to assure the poor wretches that they are not being defrauded of their allotted share of the food. I wonder if anyone dares challenge Frumley? Perhaps Rosie would. She might even, like Oliver Twist, ask for more, but no doubt she would then be punished for her impudence.

Two old women, one very bent, watched me with suspicion while they slopped water on to the filthy floor and moved it around half-heartedly with their mops. I assumed they were cleaning it. I tried to speak to them but they reacted like frightened rabbits.

Smiling, I said gently, "Please talk to me. I don't intend you any harm," but they cringed away from me and looked at each other in some alarm. Dismayed, I left them alone.

Mama says this is because they are "institutionalized" by long years confined within the repressive workhouse atmosphere. They feel uncomfortable with strangers and cannot talk naturally to them because they have nothing to say, never knowing what is going on in the world outside. They also fear to complain to visitors about their wretched conditions in case they are reported to the workhouse Master. Will this terrible system eventually grind down Rosie Chubb? I hope not and will pray for some kind of heavenly intervention on her behalf.

Friday 3rd February

Much of the snow has melted and the street sweepers are busy with their brooms. I shall be glad to see the last of it now, for so much soot has fallen from so many chimneys that the snow has become dirty and the gutters are full of melting slush.

Have stitched Theo's lace on to my blue taffeta gown as a collar and it looks very fine. We have all three been invited to the gallery in Shorne Street to see an exhibition by a young man from Holland. I do hope Mama doesn't buy another picture. The walls of the staircase are already crowded with pictures nobody actually admires, but which Mama has bought out of kindness and a desire to encourage. I shall wear the blue taffeta and my cloak with the fur-lined hood.

I find myself wondering what Rosie would look like if she were bathed in soapy water regularly, as I am, and pampered a little with creams and perfumes – and with those wild red curls brought under control. Her complexion is passable. With pretty clothes she would look quite presentable.

Oddsey, the cat, has disappeared and I am rather thankful. Prince was nervous of him and Mama none too pleased to see him, fearing that the poor animal carried disease and fleas. Most likely he has returned to the workhouse in search of Rosie. I hope he doesn't end up in Frumley's evil hands. She would be so unhappy to lose him.

Monday 6th February

Bitterly cold wind today. Glad enough to be back indoors, working on my tapestry for Mama's birthday. It is a picture of a bowl of fruit with very red apples and very orange oranges. A little too colourful, perhaps, but very striking and I think it will eventually become a cushion for her footstool. Her birthday is on the 18th of February. I pondered the date of Rosie's birth. Does she even know it? I could hardly imagine anyone in the workhouse being encouraged to celebrate a birthday. How could they? They have nothing to give. I know so little about life in the workhouse. Do they ever play games? Or sing? I must ask Mama.

My birthday is tomorrow and I wonder what Mama has bought for me? Last year it was a length of grey silk, which the dressmaker made up into a blouse. No doubt Cook will bake my favourite plum cake. She has given me a list of the ingredients and I have copied it into my book of household recipes.

Theo has gone to London to try to find work on the stage and is to meet a man who manages the Drury Lane theatre. His piano playing is good but Mama fears he is not good enough for professional work. She also hates the idea of the stage. "Hardly a suitable employment for a young man of Theo's background," she complained. He won her over, however, by hinting that he might otherwise join the Volunteers – an idea that horrified her. Thousands of young men do sign up, attracted by the uniforms, the hearty comradeship and the chance to learn to shoot a rifle. (The Volunteer Movement started in 1859 when it seemed that Napoleon the Third might threaten the British Empire.) Mama hates the idea of Theo becoming a military man.

Mrs Noye came this morning to inform Mama that Fanny Barker is very ill and asking for her. Mama was not at home, being five miles away with an invalid friend. On an impulse and in the hope of seeing Rosie again, I went instead.

I found Fanny Barker in a small room without any heating. She was shivering violently under one thin blanket and her face was chalk white. The window was wide open but when I protested, Mrs Noye said it was doctor's orders – to rid the room of any infection. Why did I doubt her explanation? I thought at once that they were hurrying the poor woman to her death deliberately – a terrible thing even to *think*.

"Is that you, Mrs Lorrimer?" Fanny asked in a quavering voice. "I wanted to thank you before—"

"I am not Mrs Lorrimer but her daughter Edith," I explained. "Mama is out of the house on an errand of mercy."

She gave a faint smile. "Your mother is a saint. If 'twere not for her sort, I should be dying in the gutter. I have escaped that shame, thank the Lord!"

But she is facing an equally shameful death in the workhouse, I thought.

"Thank her for me," the poor soul insisted, and I promised to do so.

While this was happening, Mrs Noye hovered behind me, listening to every word. She looked disapproving when I took Fanny's hand and squeezed it gently by way of farewell before leaving the room with a heavy heart.

Eager to add another chapter to Rosie's story, I asked Mrs Noye if I could see her. At first she refused, but when I insisted she led the way downstairs to an unheated basement room where five women sat on stools. They were patching blankets, though how they managed their needles with fingers clumsy with cold is a mystery. Their hands were roughened by the coarse work and made worse by the inevitable winter chilblains. Rosie, however, gave me a cheeky wink.

"This is a *great* way to pass a few hours!" she said loudly, for the benefit of Mrs Noye. "Almost as much fun as picking oakum." She grinned at me.

I stared at her, struck dumb by her dreadful appearance. Her red curls had been carelessly cropped and stood out in ugly tufts around her head.

"Don't you know what oakum is?" she went on. "Oakum's tarred rope-ends."

"Oakum?" I stammered.

"Yes. We pick the sticky ends into separate strands," she explained, "and they sell 'em to the shipyards, where some lucky men get to jam the stuff into cracks in the wooden hulls."

Mrs Noye said quickly, "It's called caulking. It

makes the ships watertight again. Most necessary. It's very useful work."

Rosie sniffed. "It's 'orrible, that oakum. Sticks to your fingers and stains 'em something chronic!"

I found my voice at last. "Rosie! Your *hair*!"

Before she could answer Mrs Noye said, "The nurse recommended it. Nits."

"Rot!" said Rosie stoutly. "It was a punishment. Oddsey came back and I was feeding him under the table. Just a few crumbs of bread." She turned to me. "They chopped off my hair – but it took three of 'em to hold me down!"

Mrs Noye had gone red in the face. "Nasty little creature! You, I mean, Chubb. You're as bad as the cat!" She turned from Rosie to me, pushing up a sleeve, to reveal a long, angry-looking scratch. "That's what she did to me!"

Rosie stabbed a finger into her hair. "And that's what *you* did to *me*, you old witch!"

The other women looked at Rosie nervously. I think they feared she would upset Mrs Noye who would then behave harshly to all of them. I wished Mama had been there. She would have known how to deal with the situation. Fortunately, perhaps because I was there, Mrs Noye did not retaliate.

I came away with one image in my mind – Rosie, clumsily shorn like a sheep, that defiant smile on her face, her green eyes glinting with anger. I imagined her kicking and screaming as they tried to apply the shears to her beautiful red curls.

Later when I told Mama about the reason for my visit, she hurried round to the workhouse with a spare blanket for Fanny. But too late. Poor Fanny was dead. When I mentioned the open window I had seen, Mama was furious. She thinks that quite likely it *was* deliberate. "One less mouth to feed," she said bitterly, and there were tears in her eyes. I wished then I had not told her.

Tuesday 7th February

My birthday. I am SIXTEEN! Prince, as usual, is wearing a birthday bow that makes him look festive. This time it is crimson. Mama gave me a beautiful gold locket, which opens to reveal a small lock of Papa's hair. Such a slender, dark curl. I had no idea that she had saved some of his hair and it touched my heart to see it. I wish I could remember him better but his image is fading and sometimes I cannot recall his voice or the way he used to laugh. I must ask Rosie about *her* parents – if she can remember them – and record the details for her in this diary. Perhaps Mama knows them.

Theo came back from London feeling disgruntled. The man from Drury Lane says he is not yet good enough to perform on the West End stage but that he does show promise and looks the part. He suggests Theo should start in the Canterbury area, where he might be promoted as "a local talent". Alternatively he should consider being an accompanist to a singer.

"Do stop sulking," I told Theo, but he pulled my hair. Great baby! Still he brought me a new bonnet for my birthday, which I shall save until Easter when I shall wear it to church and be the envy of all the women. It is dark green taffeta with pale yellow trim and a matching ribbon, which I shall tie under my chin with great pride. And yes – we did have a plum cake and I have saved a slice and will try to smuggle it in to Rosie. Amy gave me three lavender bags to put among my clothes.

It is wonderful to be sixteen. The very word has such a mature ring to it. Perhaps Theo will stop teasing me now I am no longer a child.

Wednesday 8th February

Another five inches of snow fell in the night. It is so quiet outside on the street. This morning a letter came for Cook who read it and then became quite hysterical. When Amy fetched us we found Cook with eyes already reddened from excessive weeping. Mama gave her a mouthful of brandy to revive her. When she had recovered, Cook told us that her only remaining relatives – a cousin, husband and young nephews – sailed two days ago for a new life in Australia.

"Their little smallholding has finally failed and they have so many debts, the bailiffs moved in three months ago," she explained, as fresh tears filled her eyes.

How many more people will be forced to emigrate?

Later I talked with Mama who explained the situation. Since the potato famine in Ireland in the 1840s (before I was born), thousands of small tenant farmers have had no choice but to move from their land. The Scottish highlanders have also suffered, because the rich landowners have taken away their rented land, as it is so much easier to make money from large estates. Dispossessed people still flock to England to look for employment in the towns, which are hopelessly overcrowded and work is hard to find. Even now steamships are full of emigrants who can no longer make a decent life in this country.

"But that's a shameful state of affairs!" I cried.

She shrugged. "Parliament is partly to blame," she told me. "They are constantly encouraging people to seek a fortune elsewhere in the world. The fewer people who remain in our country, the easier it will be for the government to deal with overcrowding, unemployment and poverty."

I thought about Cook while we ate our midday meal in a somewhat subdued silence. Her brother left two years ago for Australia with his wife and now the remaining members of the family have followed them. So poor Cook no longer has any family in this country. She has never been married and has no children, so the future terrifies her. What will happen to her when she is too old to work and leaves our employ?

"Surely, Mama, we could never let her go into the workhouse!"

"Certainly not, Edith. I daresay we could keep her here for her last few years and employ a new cook to come in on a daily basis."

Mama is so clever. "And will you tell Cook that? To put her mind at ease?"

She smiled. "Yes. I shall speak to her before the end of the day."

Poor Cook. It will still seem like charity (and it *will* be), but at least she will be among friends. I shall pray for her tonight, and for all the others like her. Governesses are particularly vulnerable and often end their days in the workhouse. They teach one or two generations of children and are then turned out because they are no longer needed.

Went with Theo and Mama to the art gallery in Stoneleigh to see the new exhibition, which drove out all unhappy thoughts. Theo was still sulking and walked around the gallery like a small rain cloud but I slipped on the way home and pitched headlong into the snow and that cheered him no end!

Friday 10th February

I saw Rosie again at poor Fanny Barker's funeral and asked her about her parents, but she claimed to remember very little so I shall ask Mama. It was a pauper's funeral that left much to be desired. They had put her in the cheapest available coffin. (None of the staff from the workhouse had bothered to attend.) Mama, Rosie and I walked with the sad little party, all of us ignored by most of the passers-by.

Fanny was laid to rest in an ugly corner of the churchyard among the other paupers and close to the area where suicides are buried. There the grass is never cut and the weeds flourish, particularly stinging nettles. I was glad of my long skirt, which protected my legs. There will be a simple wooden cross instead of a headstone. I asked Mama why she had not paid for a better coffin or a proper headstone, but she said it was too late to help Fanny Barker and the money would be better spent on the living.

The church service was short and hurried, and there was no music and no one to toll the bell. (When Papa was buried they tolled the bell 41 times – once for each year of his life.) Rosie was only with us because Mama had obtained permission for her to attend. For once she had little to say and seemed subdued by the occasion. She looked terrible as she stood in the snow in her shabby brown tunic. Her boots were worn (and one had lost its lace) and she had a piece of grey blanket wrapped around her shoulders to keep out the cold. I wonder if she was crushed by the thought that this would most likely be her own fate 30 years from now?

I realized with a sense of shock that probably the only time the inmates are officially allowed outside the workhouse is to attend funerals. Before we left the churchyard to return to the workhouse Mama gave us each a currant cake "by way of remembrance" and in honour of Fanny Barker. Mama told us that when her grandmother's neighbour died the mourners were given currant cakes known as "soul cakes". The currants represented the sins of the dear departed. When the cakes were eaten the sins of the dead neighbour were removed so her soul could bypass purgatory and go directly to heaven. Rosie was thrilled by this news and insisted that when *she* died we must put hundreds of currants into her soul cakes. (I think she is planning to commit a great many sins!)

I asked Rosie how Oddsey was, but she simply shrugged and appeared deep in thought. Persisting with the conversation, I asked her what she would do for the rest of the day. She replied, "I shall be working in the laundry from three 'til seven."

"And afterwards?"

She turned to me and her green eyes were dark with grief. "I shall cry myself to sleep!"

Impulsively I threw my arms around her and held her close, but after a moment she pulled herself free and stumbled away. I hoped I had not embarrassed her but Mama said later that Rosie was most likely afraid of breaking down.

"She was near to tears, Edith."

That makes two of us, I thought ruefully.

Saturday 11th February

Another sad day. I write this sitting up in bed with my candle sputtering. It will soon go out.

Just before midday Mama went into the outhouse

and found Prince asleep – as she thought. Instead my darling dog was dead. Died peacefully, Mama assured me, but it makes the loss no easier to bear. I should have been with him and I shall never forgive myself. Nor will I ever have another dog, I told her. Nothing can take Prince's place in my heart. I wish I could sleep and forget how sad I am. Even as Mama was urging me not to cry, she had tears in her own eyes. Theo buried him in the garden with his birthday ribbons and later this year I will plant some bulbs to mark his grave.

Amy says the gipsies are camped on the outskirts of town so no doubt they will be knocking on the door before long with pegs to sell. Last year one of the gipsy women told Amy's fortune by reading her palm. The gipsy said she would marry a military man within the year. Poor Amy was so excited but a year has passed and she is still with us, so perhaps the gipsy made a mistake with the date. Amy is still hopeful. The same gipsy told Cook that she was going on a sea voyage to foreign climes and poor Cook, who is terrified of the water, worried about it for months afterwards.

Thursday 16th February

Theo has been practising on the piano and I am allowed to turn the pages for him. His mood is greatly improved. He is now learning a few popular ballads to "expand his repertoire", as he explained proudly.

Mama has hired an artist to paint my portrait. The artist's name is Francis Flyte and he will make five visits. Mama had her portrait painted when she was my age but she was prettier than I am. I doubt if Rosie will ever have her portrait painted, which is a pity. With her red curls and green eyes she would look wonderful. The artist might then fall in love with her and propose! If only pigs could fly!

Friday 17th February

Mama has filled in another chapter in Rosie's story by telling me about her parents. Her father was a sailor who went to sea one day and never came back. He was drowned off the coast of Africa when his ship caught the tail end of a hurricane and foundered with all hands. Rosie's mother was expecting her second child and she and Rosie set off towards Dover to try and find her husband's parents. She went into labour while she was passing through Stoneleigh and was carried urgently to the workhouse. Both mother and baby died. Rosie, who should have had a brother, was left all alone and was taken into the workhouse. I found myself wishing I could share Theo with her.

Saturday 18th February

Another basket of oranges was delivered to the workhouse. I wonder if Rosie has had one yet or was being punished for some crime or other and denied hers…? Does she even *like* oranges? I know so little about her. I wish we could talk more often. How can I write her story when we rarely meet to exchange confidences?

Is Oddsey still alive? I often find myself thinking of Rosie and her pathetic cat. I sometimes wish I had never set foot in the workhouse because telling Rosie's story depresses me and I cannot see a way to change anything. There must be hundreds of Rosie Chubbs in hundreds of workhouses throughout this country of ours. And hundreds of Fanny Barkers buried in hundreds of pauper graves. I am so fortunate to have a happy home. I swear I will never complain again.

On a more cheerful note… Today is Mama's birthday. I gave her the tapestry and she was delighted with it, but instead of making it into a cushion for her footstool she has chosen to have the tapestry framed. Theo gave her a fur muff, which will keep her hands warm.

Secretly I wept a few private tears, reminded of the loss of my darling dog because I couldn't tie on his birthday ribbon. He is gone for ever and I miss him so much.

Mama and I went out for a walk and on the way back we saw several policeman running down an alley, blowing their whistles. We asked a passer-by what was happening and he said it was a raid on The Green Man public house, where they regularly have illegal dog fights in the cellar. Sure enough, within minutes, men were scattering in all directions in an effort to avoid arrest, but two men were marched out of the alley in handcuffs while two wretched dogs were carried out wrapped in bloodstained blankets. Their faces and paws were bloodied and torn and they looked half dead. Mama and I hurried away, unwilling, *unable*, even to speak of such an awful sight. I am so grateful that nothing so terrible ever happened to my darling Prince.

Monday 20th February

Theo had another interview this morning and has
been offered a chance to play with a violinist who is
frequently hired to perform at private parties. The pay
is very low, but Theo says he will use the work as
experience in the hope that it will pave the way to
something better. Theo is so happy, he smiles all the time.

While Mama was shopping and Theo was out I had
an unwelcome visit from Frumley. He told us Rosie
has run away from the workhouse. It seems she had
been very troublesome and had been shut in a
cupboard by way of punishment. I asked for how long
but he pretended not to know the details.

"If she comes here," he said, "you must return her to
the workhouse at once."

As he stalked away, I poked my tongue out at his
retreating back. Hateful man! But where could Rosie
have gone? I at once put on warm clothes, seized my
purse and went in search of her.

I tramped the streets, looking down every alley
where she might be lurking, but there was no sign of

her. At last I opened the door to St Mary's Church intending to pray for her safe return, but saw a small hunched figure sitting in the front pew – a solitary figure in the empty church. How typical of Rosie, to sit right at the front in someone's family pew instead of on the free seats at the back. I secretly admired her for this small gesture of defiance. As I drew nearer I heard muffled sobbing, but suddenly Rosie was alerted by my footsteps and without even pausing to see who it was, sprang to her feet and began to run towards the altar.

"It's me, Edith Lorrimer!" I called. "Wait, Rosie, please!"

She stopped and turned. Seeing me, she brushed hastily at her tearstained face and assumed her favourite expression.

"I can come to church if I like!" she declared. "It's quiet and I like the smell." She was referring to the incense. The musky perfume was certainly better than the squalid odours of the workhouse. She went on, "Nothing to do with you where I go or what I do!"

I took a few hesitant steps towards her, for she reminded me of a startled deer poised for flight. Perhaps this was the chance I had been waiting for – the chance to talk with her and learn more of her story. "I was worried about you, Rosie," I told her quietly.

"Frumley said you had … you were missing. I thought you might have come to some harm and needed help."

"Well, I haven't and I don't!"

I sat down and after a moment's indecision Rosie did the same. I learned that she had been kept in the broom cupboard for four hours – a stiflingly small cupboard full of mops and buckets. And her crime? She had tried to defend one of the old women who was being insulted by Mrs Noye.

"One day I'll run away and never go back," she told me. "I'll never set foot in that evil, stinking place ever again. I'm just biding my time."

"What made you come here, Rosie?" I asked, genuinely curious. "Does it comfort you to sit in God's house?"

"It comforts me to be out of the cold!" She tossed her head.

"Do you go to the chapel in the … where you live?"

"Sometimes … but not when there's a service. I creep in there sometimes to be alone. It's peaceful."

I longed to comfort her but remembered my last attempt in the churchyard and was fearful of driving her away. Did anyone ever show her kindness or affection? Instead I said, "We could pray together if you wish."

We did so but silently and I have no idea what Rosie prayed for – unless it was for a miracle.

When we left the church I took her to a stall that sold mutton pies and bought her one. I watched appalled as she gobbled it down like a starving animal so I bought her another and watched her devour it with the same speed. I wanted to give her quince tart, fruit jelly, smoked ham, truffles, iced cake, syllabub, roast beef, cherry cake, strawberries and cream and so much more! Instead I bought her a mug of tea.

I took her back to our house but she refused to come in. Mama was home by then and returned with her to the workhouse in the hope that Rosie would escape further punishment. But first we found her some decent boots – a little big for her (they were once Theo's), but Rosie was delighted with them.

After she and Mama had gone, I burst into tears for no real reason.

"Rosie Chubb," I whispered. "Whatever will become of you?"

Afterwards Theo and I talked about what could be done for her and he suggested we try to find her a job. I came up to bed feeling a little happier.

Thursday 23rd February

Today's Board Meeting was in the morning and started at ten o'clock. A young woman with a baby who lived locally was applying for "outdoor relief". Joan Petty and her infant Billy. She refused point-blank to "take the house". (In other words, she would not accept indoor relief.) What she wanted was a temporary solution to what should be a short-lived problem. She would live outside the workhouse resuming her former life as far as possible. Joan Petty desperately wanted to remain independent and to keep her son out of the workhouse – and who could blame her? Frumley asked if she had a room to go to and she said, "Yes."

"Are you a married woman?"

She nodded, but went on, "But he's dead – a week ago." He mouth trembled. "He was set upon by three young bullies who—"

"No need for all that," Frumley snapped. "Did he have a trade?"

She explained that her husband had been a knife

grinder and I realized at once that Mr Petty must have sharpened our knives many times over the past years. He'd do his rounds, pushing his small cart and playing his penny whistle to alert the housewives to his presence. I remembered him as a shy man, painfully thin, but a cheerful worker. Cook always claimed he did a good job with the knives.

Joan Petty continued, "We have an attic room over the cobbler's shop in the High Street but without my husband's money I cannot pay the rent."

Frumley tutted, as though this was a poor excuse. "So how will you and the child live now, if you don't come into the workhouse? We won't pay your rent indefinitely."

"I'll find something to do. Washing, cleaning…" She glanced down at the sleeping baby and fussed with the meagre shawl in which young Billy was wrapped. "It's just to tide us over the next week. A shilling or two…"

Mama said, "Where will you and your baby sleep tonight if Mr Frumley doesn't help you?"

"We'll find somewhere. A barn with some straw." She shrugged.

Frumley glared at her. "Last time we gave your sort outdoor relief she spent the money on drink. We found her two hours later in a doorway sodden with gin."

To my surprise, Mrs Noye interrupted him. "I'm sure Mrs Petty would do no such thing. She has a child to think about."

We all looked at the workhouse Master. "Four days' rent," he said grudgingly. "Take it or leave it."

"But … we must eat."

As though the desperate situation had somehow penetrated the baby's dreams, Billy suddenly awoke and began to cry. Mrs Pleshey said she would give the woman a shilling for food. Joan Petty accepted the offer gratefully and hurried from the room before Frumley could change his mind.

I found myself fuming at Frumley's cruel words. "What do you mean by 'your sort'?" I demanded angrily. "She is just a poor unhappy widow doing what is best for her child. How could you suggest she drinks?"

Frumley's eyes blazed as he looked at me and he puffed up so with anger that I hoped he would burst a button – but no such luck.

"Don't be so gullible, Miss Lorrimer!" he snapped. "She is nothing but a fallen woman."

"But she is a *widow*," Mrs Pleshey argued.

"Widow? Poppycock! I doubt the wretched woman is telling the truth about this 'husband' of hers. Probably no better than she should be and has had the child out of wedlock! People who offend against the Lord deserve no pity."

I was astonished. People are such hypocrites. Last year I read the novel *Ruth*, written by Mrs Gaskell (and recommended by Mama, who thought I should understand what a wicked place the world can be for the unwary!). It tells of a poor young woman who is seduced by a man who then abandons her. It made sad but compelling reading and was widely praised, but Mama says it was banned from several private lending libraries as "likely to corrupt".

Mrs Noye's face had reddened. "The Master knows what is best, Miss Lorrimer. He has years of experience. You should remember that."

I opened my mouth to protest further but Mrs Pleshey then spoke up for me, saying that we should always think the best of applicants and not the worst. For a long moment Frumley simply stared at his pen, then abruptly announced that they would move to item one on the agenda.

The Board then discussed various matters. A latch needed replacing on the door to Frumley's office. The cook claimed that the butcher was not delivering as much mutton as previously, but was charging the same price. There was a need for new undergarments for some of the women and a rat-catcher had been called in to deal with vermin and had sent an exorbitant bill for which there were no spare funds. Mrs Pleshey said she would pay it and opened her purse. I saw a fleeting smile touch Frumley's lips and of a sudden I was suspicious.

"May I see the invoice?" I asked brightly. "Mama insists that I take a close interest in such matters." They were all staring at me again, including Mama.

"I'm here to learn," I insisted innocently, though I was beginning to regret the impulsive enquiry.

Frumley said quickly that he had mislaid it but knew the exact amount and Mrs Pleshey at once counted the coins into his outstretched hand.

Then we were taken to see the new blankets, which Leonard Price had provided for the men's dormitory. It seems that a month earlier he had done the same for the women.

As we followed Mrs Noye along the corridors we passed Rosie, who was barefooted. She turned her head and hissed, "Don't believe all you see!"

I wondered what to make of this remark, but there was no time to ask. We duly admired the new blankets in the men's dormitory and Mama congratulated Leonard Price on his generosity. The dormitory was freezing cold and the fireplace boasted nothing but a few very dead coals.

There were twenty truckle beds in the room and a wooden chair beside each one. There were no rugs on the tiled floor and the two large windows were open.

I imagined the men trying to sleep while snowflakes whirled in and settled around their sleeping forms. If they *were* able to sleep in such conditions. Did any of them die of cold? I wondered uneasily.

We returned to the corridor and Mama drew Mrs Noye aside and asked why Rosie was not wearing the boots we had given her. It was, Mrs Noye explained smugly, to stop her running away again.

"You mean it is a punishment?"

"No. It's to stop her going off again. She can't run away in her bare feet!"

"But the floors are so cold," Mrs Pleshey protested. "She will catch a chill!"

"Mr Frumley's orders!"

As we headed for the stairs I felt a hand clutch at my sleeve and allowed myself to be drawn aside into an alcove out of sight. It was Rosie again. She put a finger to her lips and led me to the women's dormitory. The beds were covered with threadbare blankets.

"But where—?" I began, confused.

"They're on the men's beds! Work it out for yourself. Now go!"

I hurried after the rest of the Board members, my mind racing. Frumley had only bought *one* set of blankets, but had accepted the money for two sets. My heart began to thump with anger. It was a cruel and deliberate fraud. I waited impatiently for the chance to tell Mama.

Friday 24th February

Said nothing yesterday to Mama about the blankets because I needed to think things through. I was new to the workhouse and its workings and feared to rush in with false accusations. I lay awake for hours last night and became even more suspicious. Had they, in fact, called in a rat-catcher? Was that another fraud? Was Alfred Frumley cheating on a large scale? Was he making fools of the authorities as well as the well-meaning Board members who were trying so hard to make a difference to the lives of the unhappy men and women within the workhouse walls?

I recalled the oranges Mama donates each week. And every winter the Board members contribute to a fund to buy extra coal when the snow arrives. There had been a decent fire in the office. But elsewhere?

I decided I must speak out. Mama listened to me in silence as I told her about Rosie and the missing blankets. "There must be an explanation," she said at last. "Perhaps the blankets were being washed."

"But they were almost new. Bought just over a month ago. They wouldn't need washing already."

She hesitated, unwilling to believe that I might be right. "Rosie might be lying," she said slowly. "She hates Alfred Frumley ... and he did say she was a troublemaker."

"We could demand to see the blankets."

"We would have to explain why... And they were given by Leonard Price. It would be up to him." She looked worried. "It's a very serious accusation and it involves Rosie. Oh dear!" She put a hand to her head and I at once regretted alarming her.

"Let's say nothing at present," I suggested, "but be aware that he might not be trustworthy."

We left it like that, but I made up my mind that I would somehow talk with Rosie and learn more.

Monday 27th February

Theo has come up with a clever idea, which is that I should teach Rosie to read and write. This should be done once a week at our house. Have put the idea to Mama who gave it cautious approval. Cautious because it will be unfair on the other inmates and they might become envious of Rosie. Why is it so difficult to help people?

Many of the long-term residents will have received only the most basic education, which the workhouse tries to provide. At present there is no teacher, the last one having given up the thankless task many months ago. Apparently she complained about the harsh conditions, the apathy of her pupils, the inadequate resources and poor pay, and finally she went home to nurse her aged mother.

Mama told me not to be too hopeful. Most of the inmates regularly played truant from the lessons, disliking yet more discipline. No doubt Rosie was one of the rebellious ones, I thought. The workhouse Master will certainly oppose the idea on principle and will hate the idea that Rosie is bettering herself. But we must at least try. I was becoming frustrated. More than anything I wanted something positive to happen for Rosie. So far all I have written is a story of her trials and tribulations.

"If we can help get her out of there it will be a triumph!" Theo argued. "In fact it will be a miracle! Most people leave the workhouse in a cheap coffin!"

That careless jibe hit home, for both Mama and I immediately recalled poor Fanny Barker.

Wednesday 1st March

As expected, Frumley objected strongly to the idea of Rosie spending a few hours with us being educated when she should be patching blankets or picking the horrible oakum. He argued that she would have to forfeit one of her meals. Mama countered that Rosie would eat one meal with us. Eventually, reluctantly, he agreed. This morning Rosie was actually allowed out of the workhouse and by ten past eleven this morning she was at our front door. When she came in we saw at once that she was dirtier than usual.

"The miserable pig said I 'ad to do my share of the work first," she explained indignantly, "so I was got up extra early and ordered to scrub the kitchen floor, which made the cook mad 'cos I was under 'er feet all the time. Then she slipped on the soap and blamed me. Said I did it on purpose – which I never did…" She faltered to a halt, blinking back unfamiliar tears. I was lost for words to comfort her, but Mama was wonderful.

"I thought you might like a bath, Rosie," she said cheerfully. "The hot water is ready and a tin bath is in the outhouse waiting for you with soap and flannel. I'll put some perfumed oil in the water and you'll be cosy and private."

She was as good as her word and soon Rosie was enjoying the luxury of a good hot bath – probably the first she had ever had in her life. We left her in peace with a large fluffy towel. Mama suggested she might also want to wash her hair. Meanwhile Rosie's clothes were sponged clean and hung up to dry and some spare clothes were found for her.

When she reappeared we all stared at the transformation and I took her up to my bedroom so that she could see herself in the mirror. Later Theo came home from a visit to the tailor and was visibly impressed by the young redheaded creature, who was by then earnestly scratching away on a slate with a slate pencil.

He went into the parlour to practise his music, Mama went to see Mrs Pleshey and I answered the door to the coalman. When I returned I was surprised to hear Rosie, still bent over her slate, singing along to one of Theo's ballads.

"You know the song?" I asked. Surely she had never been to a music hall.

"I know lots of songs. Old Marie at the workhouse taught me 'em. She used to be a singer till she got ill with 'er throat and lost 'er voice. That's 'ow come she got in the workhouse. All she could do was croak but she remembered the words. Dead now, poor thing. The pneumonia took her... There! 'Ow's that for a bit of writing?" She handed me the slate on which she had managed a few shaky letters. A capital A, T, F and L which she had copied from mine. I thought, being straight letters, she would find them easier than the rounded ones.

"Bit wobbly," she admitted, "but there's something wrong with this slate thing." She gave the slate pencil a stern look.

"You've done well."

"Am I done, then?" Rosie slid from the chair, apparently under the impression that the lesson was over.

"Not yet," I told her quickly. "I want you to try some more letters. I want you to write your name. Look. Watch carefully. R-O-S-I-E."

She tried to copy them, but her concentration wandered and after her third attempt she tossed the slate aside and announced that the lesson was over.

"Why don't you show Theo how you wrote your name?" I suggested.

She was off in a flash to the next room with the slate in her hand. When I followed her a little later I found her watching Theo play. She had a rapt expression on her face and the slate was abandoned on a nearby table.

Later, after eating an enormous meal of cold bacon and pickles, Rosie once more donned her scratchy uniform, pulled the shawl close round her shoulders and prepared to return to the hell of the workhouse. To my surprise, Theo offered to accompany her. Wonders will never cease, I thought, as I helped Mama to empty the big tin bath and tidy up the outhouse.

"So did you learn any more about Alfred Frumley and the missing blankets?" Mama asked as I mopped up spilled soapsuds.

Embarrassed, I shook my head. In the excitement of having Rosie in the house, I had quite forgotten to ask; but at least I have something happy to write about Rosie in my diary.

Thursday 2nd March

Today's Board Meeting started a quarter of an hour late, as the workhouse had been the subject of an unannounced inspection from the authorities. As soon as we were seated at the long oak table, a Dr Ambrose from the Local Government Board was introduced to us. Not a medical man, apparently, but a doctor of philosophy, whatever that may be. He was a stout, bewhiskered man with brown eyes that glittered behind small spectacles. I at once caught Mama's gaze and we were both wondering if he had discovered any financial irregularities in the Stoneleigh Workhouse records.

He announced that he wished to interview Lizzie Harrold, one of the residents. The poor woman was obviously nervous as she came into the room and stood before us, anxiously twisting her hands. Her brown dress was too long and the hem had been clumsily raised. Beneath her bonnet, sparse grey hair was scraped back into a bun and fixed with large hairpins. Clutching her shawl, she looked round at us with a trusting, childlike smile. Dr Ambrose asked her if she had any money to pay for her funeral. She brightened and nodded vigorously. I saw at once that she had been tricked.

"Tell Mr Frumley where this money is kept."

Now she also saw it and hesitated. "'Tis sewn into my mattress, Mr Frumley, sir … but I didn't mean no harm. I can't abear the thought of a pauper's burial."

Dr Ambrose turned to look enquiringly at Frumley who jumped to his feet, enraged, and demanded to know where the money had come from, reminding her about the rules that stated all money should be declared when asking for indoor relief.

"I didn't have it then, Mr Frumley, sir. I … I found it."

"*Found* it? You *found* money just lying around?" He glared at her. "You don't know whose it was, and you didn't hand it in? Surely you knew it wasn't yours."

"I'm ever so sorry, Mr Frumley, sir!" Lizzie's face now crumpled and my heart ached for the poor soul. But where *had* the money come from?

"I didn't mean any harm." Tears rolled down her face.

Leonard Price said, "You mustn't bully the poor woman, Mr Frumley. I'm sure she will hand over the money if you ask her nicely."

Poor Lizzie dabbed at her tears with the end of her shawl. "'Twas Rosie that gave it me. She knew as I was fearful, being a pauper."

So now Rosie was under scrutiny – for where had *she* found money unless it was stolen? Mama groaned and Frumley hastily decided the matter should be dealt with elsewhere. He glanced at the visiting inspector, then back at the shivering woman. "Go with Mrs Noye, find the money and hand it over. I'll talk to you later."

"But, sir, *please*..." More tears. "I beg you, kind sir..."

But Frumley was not a "kind sir". He signalled to Mrs Noye, who rose to her feet and pushed Lizzie Harrold from the room.

Mama said, "Is it not possible for the money to be set aside for her funeral?"

Dr Ambrose frowned. "Certainly not. It would encourage others to try to cheat the system. People applying for relief of any kind have to prove that they are destitute. In some workhouses she would be thrown back onto the streets for her deceit."

"But not from Stoneleigh Workhouse." Mrs Pleshey gave him a stern look.

"We shall have to see," Dr Ambrose told her. "My job is to see that the funds are properly used and the workhouses correctly administered."

He then announced that he would sit with us through the rest of the agenda and we began the meeting proper. The first item was Rosie's absence from the building when she came to our house for her writing lesson. Frumley told everyone that it had aroused so much envy among the others that in future no more visits would be allowed.

Without thinking I protested, "But I am teaching her to read and write. That will surely be to her advantage."

Mama said quickly, "Perhaps Edith could come to the workhouse and teach all the residents – or at least the women. Then there would be no envy."

Out of the question, we were told. The inmates have no time for such luxuries. They have their work to do.

Item two was a further request to the Board to pay for the doctor who had called to see one of the inmates. Mama asked to see the invoice but was told it was not available. Dr Ambrose said, "Perhaps *I* may see it before I leave."

Frumley reddened and began to stammer, and Mrs Noye looked frightened. I wondered what Frumley would do if there was no such invoice. *Had* the local doctor been called? I doubted it.

Friday 3rd March

Another cold day. Strong winds from the east. Good news about Theo. He has a possible musical engagement and is very excited.

Not such good news about Mama who has lost a ring that was her mother's and she suspects Rosie has taken it. Is it possible Rosie is the thief? Even I think it is. But how can we ask her without insulting her? And what can she do with it? If she tries to sell it she will arouse suspicion and she dare not wear it.

And worse news for poor Cook. She tripped on the stairs yesterday and hurt her back, so Mama has set her to polishing the cutlery so that she can sit down, and is spending more time in the kitchen herself.

Mama had a letter for Mrs Noye, so asked me to take it to the workhouse in her stead. I was happy to go, as I hoped I might see Rosie. Also I do not care for cooking and suspect that, with Cook disabled, I would be expected to help out with the vegetables for a hearty mutton stew. Mama also pretends I have a light hand for making dumplings.

I arrived at the workhouse soon after ten o'clock and a mighty hammering and clanging at once assailed my ears. I realized that the noise was coming from the stone-breaking which is a part of the men's labour each day. Full of curiosity, I delivered Mama's letter to the office and crept round to see what was happening. The door was ajar and I saw a small group of shabbily dressed men sitting at intervals from each other on a bench. If they had washed that morning it wasn't obvious from their appearance. In front of them, set into the earth floor, was a long rectangular iron grid, which was covered with large stones of various shapes. I assumed that the grid was set above a cellar. Each man hefted a heavy mallet and with this he smashed the stones on the grid in front of him. As the stone crumbled the smaller pieces fell through the grid. A large pile of stones waited nearby and, as I watched, one of the men left his seat and took up a shovel with which to replenish the stones above the grid. Small chips flew in all directions. The men worked in silence, for no conversation could possibly survive in that hellish din. I covered my ears with my hands but my whole body was shaken by the vibrations caused by mallets on stone and metal.

One of the men caught sight of me and at once alerted the others who stopped working, no doubt thankful for any excuse. Finding myself the centre of unwanted attention, I said, "What happens to the stones once they are broken up?"

One of them, a burly man, said, "The workhouse sells them. They go to make the roads. Want a try?" He grinned through gappy teeth. "Young Rosie had a go last summer. Dropped the mallet on her toe and was hobbling around for weeks!"

They all found this memory hilarious.

"I doubt I could even lift the mallet," I said hastily and they liked that comment.

A small man pointed to his face and I saw that he wore a black patch over one eye. "Splinter," he explained, and my blood ran cold at the thought of a stone chip in a man's eye. I looked at each of them and saw one elderly man with a scar on his cheek.

"That also?" I asked, but he shook his head. He had been in a fight in the casual ward, he told me. His account was chilling. A few years ago he had come into the workhouse as a "casual" as he passed through Stoneleigh on his way to Whitstable, where his uncle had three months' work for him cleaning and carting shellfish. "Mostly oysters," he grinned. "Lovely, they are, Whitstable oysters. Slip down your throat like wine, they do!"

The casual ward is a separate dormitory for passing labourers on the move from one place to another. I had seen it in daytime with its rows of so-called beds (they look like wooden troughs), which are available for men who have nowhere better to stay. There are no mattresses, for they are too easily stolen, and no pillows. The men carry a blanket roll and cover themselves with this and rest their heads on the bags they carry. Most men are too weary to care and can sleep without luxuries. They come in after eight at night and either pay a few coppers or work at stone-breaking the next morning. A dish of thin oatmeal is included as breakfast.

"I was minding my own business," the man went on. "Around nine it was, and getting dark, when this chap come up to me and said I was to give him half my bread. Well, I'd been given it by some old dear when I knocked on her back door that afternoon and had stuffed it in me pocket for supper, so to speak. When I refused to share, he snatched it and I snatched it back, and then everyone was piling in and I got kicked in the face. The doctor had to put in five stitches to stop the bleeding."

This evening I was rereading *Uncle Tom's Cabin* about the slaves in America before the Civil War and thought about whether I should try to write a novel. The Brontë sisters started their writing at a very early age, so why shouldn't I? I wondered if Harriet Beecher Stowe had seen the slaves for herself and whether or not she had exaggerated their plight. Probably not, I decided, comparing their existence to that of the unfortunates in the workhouse. Life can be almost unbearable for the poor and lowly, wherever they live. True, in our workhouses they are not being bought and sold but they are scarcely better off, for they are no longer in control of their own destinies. Not for the first time I felt angry with Queen Victoria, safely tucked away on the Isle of Wight mourning her beloved Prince Albert. She should come back to London and live in the real world and see the plight of some of her subjects.

Saturday 4th March

Theo's first musical engagement has been confirmed! It's at the end of next week. He will be playing a Chopin sonata with a violinist and also accompanying a young tenor who will sing three pieces from Schubert. The audience will be members of the Stoneleigh Music Appreciation Society and the event, their annual Gala Night. It all sounds very grand. Theo will be paid the handsome sum of one guinea.

More trouble to recount in the ongoing story of Rosie Chubb! The mystery of the missing ring has been solved. Old Mr Arbuthnot from the jewellers in the High Street called on us this morning. He told us that a young woman had taken a ring to him to sell, claiming that she had a dying mother and needed the money for medicines. He recognized it as a ring his father had made years ago for my grandmother and was immediately suspicious. He refused to buy it and believes she was then going to a pawnbroker. The young woman had curly red hair. Obviously Rosie. What a catastrophe.

Mama visited the pawnbroker, recognized the ring and is going to buy it back if it is not redeemed by Rosie within the required time.

Sunday 5th March

Theo is practising hard for his debut. Mama and I have bought tickets for the event. Theo has a new black suit for the occasion, with narrow trouser legs, as is the fashion. He is so vain. He still asks about Rosie. I think he is as intrigued with her as I am. Poor Rosie. Who will love her? A workhouse girl has no prospects of marriage and family. She has no education, no household skills (unless you include scrubbing floors and patching blankets) and no creative talent that we can see.

Saturday 11th March

Theo's concert went well. His playing was received with loud applause and he only stumbled once during his accompaniment, and that was when the pages were turned incorrectly. Mama and I were very proud of him.

In the interval we drank champagne and nibbled petits fours. Then we listened to a small choir and two songs from a plump soprano, whose name I forget. Afterwards a man approached Theo and they discussed a private soiree and Theo was offered more work. It is most gratifying.

Tuesday 14th March

Sunshine at last. I was feeling truly cheerful this morning until Mama and I went to the market and a young thief stole Mama's purse. Snatched it from her hand as cheeky as you like and ran off laughing. Several men went after him and he was caught and held. But by then he had "lost" the purse – passed it to an accomplice, most likely. There was no proof that he was the villain, except that I was a witness and declared him so.

A constable took him away. As he was dragged off he looked me straight in the eyes and shouted, "Rosie won't be very 'appy!"

I was dumbstruck. Rosie and this thief? Was she getting into bad company? My heart sank. Suppose she ends up in a prison cell? It would be marginally worse than the workhouse!

We discovered the boy's name, which was Jake, and determined to question Rosie about him. But we have to do so without alerting Frumley or Mrs Noye, for they would no doubt use the knowledge against Rosie.

Thursday 16th March

On arriving at the Board Meeting I was told by Mrs Noye that Joan Petty had been found dead in her room over the cobbler's shop and that the baby Billy had been accepted into Stoneleigh Workhouse. The news saddened me, but there was nothing I could do and I had something else on my mind. I pretended that I had lost my handkerchief and slipped out to go in search of it. In fact I had deliberately tossed it into a dark corner on my way in. I left the boardroom and hurried along the corridor, safe in the knowledge that Frumley and Mrs Noye were at the meeting.

I found Rosie struggling with the dreaded oakum, (along with six others), her fingers stained and bleeding from the coarse rope strands. As she was unsupervised, I was able to take her to one side where the other women could not overhear us.

"Who's Jake?" I asked.

A broad smile lit up her face. "Mind your own business!"

"He's been arrested."

Her face fell. "Oh Gawd! What did he do?"

"Stole Mama's purse. And Mama's ring has also disappeared. She is broken-hearted, poor soul."

Rosie's face reddened and her guilt was clear, as she avoided my eyes. After several clumsy lies she finally confessed. It turns out that she met Jake when he called at the workhouse to visit his grandfather. Rosie imagines they are in love and is trying to help him.

"He needs a few readies," she told me earnestly. "I only pawned the ring. Jake's saving the money to buy me a mangle so I can leave here and work for my living."

This means she would take in people's ready-washed linen and mangle the water from it. Properly done, this makes the sheets easier to dry and they need little ironing, but it is poorly paid work.

Rosie went on. "Jake's a poppet and 'e's mad with love for me!"

I doubted it. More likely using her, I thought sadly, and spending the money. How does she know who she can trust? But I daresay if I were in her shoes I would take any risk if I thought I could leave the horrors of the workhouse behind me. Especially if I thought someone loved me!

"Did you give some of the ring money to Lizzie Harrold?"

She rolled her eyes. "Lizzie was always droning on about her poxy funeral so I gave her a couple of shillings to shut her up. Much good it did. For my sins I got no dinner, the money's gone and Lizzie's still moaning!"

I also asked her about the new blankets and it seems they have now all vanished. I rushed to look in at both dormitories and found it so.

When I returned to the meeting Frumley looked at me suspiciously.

"Where have you been all this time, Miss Lorrimer?"

"I couldn't find my handkerchief, but now I have it." I produced it by way of confirmation. He exchanged a look with Mrs Noye and I knew he wasn't convinced. So now *I* am lying! It must be contagious.

Monday 20th March

Mr Flyte, the artist, came this morning to begin work on my portrait which was a big excitement. I wore my lavender jacket and skirt and he insisted I wore a bonnet.

"To add to the impression of modesty," he explained.

He suggested I held an open bible – in an attempt to appear God-fearing – but then he changed his mind and wanted a piece of sewing instead.

"To add to the impression of industry?" I asked, tongue in cheek

He simply agreed, pleased that I was beginning to understand his way of thinking. He is a large man with a florid complexion, not at all how I had imagined him to be. (A slim man with dark curls and flashing eyes would have been my choice.) Mr Flyte made several sketches with his charcoal and talked interminably about his other – more important – sitters. Unimpressed with the sketches, I fear for the finished likeness.

I have just finished reading *Great Expectations* by Charles Dickens and think Miss Haversham the most wonderfully drawn character, and the decaying wedding cake *so* sad. How does an author learn the tricks of his trade, I wonder? Mr Dickens learned his from personal experience from the hardships of his youth. I have heard it said that for a while, when young, he worked in a blacking factory. Could *I* write a novel? I am still toying with the idea. When I spoke of it to Mama she was interested in the idea, but asked me what I would write about. "Why, Stoneleigh Workhouse!" I told her.

Tuesday 21st March

I witnessed a most terrible scene today in the workhouse and pray never to see the like again. Mama and I called in unexpectedly to take some hard-boiled eggs for the seven young children who live there. I understand that there are only a few children at Stoneleigh Workhouse because there is a large orphanage six miles away where most of them are sent. We had decorated the eggs by boiling them in water containing onion skins which somehow creates interesting brown patterns on the shells. We had scarce been in the workhouse five minutes and were still speaking to Mrs Noye when a great commotion broke out at the end of the downstairs corridor.

She said, "Oh no! It's the lunatic!"

Crashes and screams and shouted oaths made us forget everything, and we all ran towards the sounds. The women's day room was the source of the noise and there we found a dozen or more women huddled together at one end of the room, while two of the women tried unsuccessfully to subdue a large man.

This wretched creature, whose name was Will Warton, might well have qualified for the "wild man from Borneo" himself! He was heavily built and wore ragged clothes, which appeared to be made from sacking. His eyes were wild, his hair long and tangled and a bushy beard hid much of his face. Foam flecked his lips as he threw one of his attackers to the ground. "Lucy!" he bellowed. "Where are you? *Lucy*!"

Mrs Noye muttered, "Not the invisible Lucy again!" and sent one of the cowering women in search of Frumley. As the crazed man rushed towards the huddled women they scattered like leaves in a breeze, and he crashed into the wall and collapsed onto the floor. There he sat, sobbing and rocking to and fro, calling from time to time for "Lucy". To my surprise, Rosie at once sat down beside him, patting his hand in an effort to comfort him. He turned his shaggy head towards her, mumbling despairingly. She smiled at him then slipped her arm round his shoulder.

"Will he hurt her?" I asked nervously. If he turned on Rosie she would be in real danger.

Mrs Noye shook her head. "He trusts Chubb – Lord knows why!"

"What is wrong with him?" Mama demanded. "Who is Lucy?"

We watched for a moment as Will Warton continued his incoherent lament. Speaking to him soothingly, Rosie reached up and wiped his tears away with her fingers. She turned briefly, caught my eye and smiled faintly.

As I forced back tears Mrs Noye explained that Will Warton is insane but there is no room for him in the county asylum which is based on the famous Colney Hatch asylum in London. They were all built to offer shelter to pauper lunatics. "Sadly all the asylums have a long waiting list of deserving cases," she told us. "It's a big step in the right direction but the authorities have built too few of them."

When Will was certified as insane there was nowhere else for him to go except Stoneleigh Workhouse.

"He suffers from severe delusions," Mrs Noye sighed. "He was a much nicer person when he first came to us but over the last three years he has been rapidly deteriorating. He is always looking for his wife Lucy and believes she is being kept away from him."

"And is she?" I demanded, expecting this to be the case, but I was wrong.

Poor Will Warton has never been married, having been of unsound mind even as a child. He was labelled an imbecile but, being very peaceable, had been kindly tolerated by his neighbours as "the village idiot". When his parents died he soon became destitute.

Mama was obviously shaken by this story. "Why haven't we seen him before?"

"He has to be locked up away from the other inmates."

We learned that Will Warton had on occasions become hostile to those around him. He regularly tore up his clothes and refused to let anyone near to wash him or trim his hair or beard.

"The new asylums have better ways to deal with such people," Mrs Noye told us wearily. "The authorities give the lunatic asylums more money. They have more suitable accommodation, more secure premises and specially qualified doctors. You cannot blame us."

One by one the women were slipping from the room, escaping from the unhappy scene to make their way up to the relative safety of their dormitory. I imagined they would wait there until Will Warton was once more locked away.

I asked when that would be. "As soon as he has calmed down. Then he will give in as meek as a lamb. You'll see."

We did. After we had visited the children and given them their eggs we returned to the women's day room. Will had slumped to the floor and was curled up like a child, sucking his thumb. Rosie was gone. Frumley arrived with the local doctor who walked confidently towards Will Warton.

He held out his hand. "Come along, Mr Warton," he said cheerfully. "Lucy is upstairs, waiting for you."

Will struggled eagerly to his feet and took the doctor's hand. They left the room with Mrs Noye a few steps behind them and Mama and I heard them mount the stone steps. After a moment there was a brief scuffle and then a door slammed. Outside in the corridor we listened and heard a loud hammering, screams and shouts of anger. The doctor and Mrs Noye rejoined us, looking chastened.

White-faced, Mama whispered, "That was terrible!"

The doctor nodded. He looked defeated. "What else can we do for him here? He'll be given a strong sleeping draught. While he's asleep they will do what they can to wash him and tidy him up."

Before we left the workhouse we were taken back to Will Warton's room to see for ourselves what had happened to him. His room was very small and dingy. The furniture consisted of a mattress on the floor on which he was sleeping. The walls were bare, there was no window and the air smelled stale. His hair and beard had been trimmed and he looked strangely childlike in sleep. I asked what he did all day and Mrs Noye shrugged. "Talks to himself a lot."

I thought that if I were locked up alone in that dismal room all day I would soon be as mad as Will Warton.

Mama looked shocked. "Doesn't he have any outside exercise?"

Once a week was her answer. "But never in the company of others. He's too unpredictable."

This evening Mama and I were understandably subdued and I have learned a hard truth. There is no way, with all the goodwill in the world, that we can solve all the world's ills.

Wednesday 22nd March

I found it hard to sleep last night and when I did I dreamed about Will Warton. He was wandering alone in a dark forest, lumbering from tree to tree in search of the comforting presence of the non-existent Lucy, while the moonlight cast his shadow behind him like a lonely ghost.

Awoke with a stomach ache so have stayed in bed today. Mama was none too well either and blamed the pigeons in the pie we had for dinner. She thought they smelled suspiciously "high" when they first came out of the larder but Cook washed them in vinegar water and declared them "quite fit to eat". Perhaps she was wrong.

Thankfully Mama was feeling much better later. She went out and bought back her ring and will say no more about the matter. She has written a letter to Dr Ambrose making an official request that I may spend a little time in the workhouse teaching some of them – perhaps the brightest – to read and write. If he agrees Frumley will be overruled. He will not take kindly to Mama's interference but will be helpless to prevent it.

Leonard Price came round, and he and Mama discussed the new blankets and he is going to ask to see both dormitories. I do believe we shall find that Frumley has sold them and put the money in his own pocket.

A constable called also to make enquiries about Jake. The wretch is still denying that he took anything and will not name his accomplice. Mama, soft-hearted as ever, asked that Jake be given one more chance to mend his ways. It seems he is only seventeen, but looks much older.

Thursday 23rd March

Recovered from my stomach disorder but today Mama has insisted I shall not go with her to the workhouse. So I shall miss the excitement when Leonard Price asks to see the blankets.

When Amy returned from shopping this morning she said there was a dancing bear in the town centre.

"He was up on his hind legs," she told me breathlessly, "and was taller than the man who owned him. He had a ring through his nose and the man held him on a chain and when he started to whistle the bear danced. You should have been there! It was wonderful!"

Amy has all the fun, I thought enviously, but merely said "Poor thing!" in what I hoped was a lofty tone. Last year on May Day she went to the fair on the common, but Mama refused to let me go with her as she says the showmen are little better than rogues and it is no place for a well-bred young woman. Amy saw wondrous sights – the fattest lady in the world, the smallest man and a dog with two heads. She also won a goldfish in a jar, but the next morning it was dead.

I spent the morning reading *Alice In Wonderland* by Lewis Carroll, which everyone rates highly – but it is a strange story.

This evening brought more bad news. Frumley finally allowed Leonard Price to visit the dormitories. There were no new blankets but Frumley had invented an excuse. He claimed that they were at the laundry having name tags stitched into them. He's as crafty as a cartload of monkeys.

Saturday 25th March

Jake has been released from custody. Mama was hoping to speak with him about his bad ways but he has gone to ground like a fox. He will certainly go to prison if he is arrested again.

I gave three pence to a man who was begging outside the bakery where they make the mutton pies. He was eager to talk and told me he was a horseman by trade but the farmer who employed him bought a newfangled steam tractor so no longer needed men or horses. It seems the steam tractor is a noisy clanking contraption with iron wheels, an engine and a chimney. Could it possibly become popular with farmers? Surely it would terrify the livestock and deafen the driver. And I cannot imagine a world without horses. What would happen to them all? Cook thinks they would be slaughtered and turned into cats' meat! What a terrible thought.

Monday 27th March

Francis Flyte came again and this time in earnest. He brought an easel, a palette, tubes of paint and a number of brushes. He tells me he is going to concentrate on my face and hands, and will later fill in the clothes and background from his sketches.

Oddsey appeared in our garden this morning without warning. Mama thinks maybe Jake brought the cat round on Rosie's behalf. We fed the cat and gave him a saucer of milk but he disappeared again. Seeing him reminded me of poor Prince. Theo has made a small wooden cross for his grave. On this he has burned the name "PRINCE" with a hot poker.

Tuesday 28th March

Two letters this morning. One from Leonard Price saying that the laundry had no knowledge of the blankets and he will contact the Local Government Board to ask for an investigation. Another from Dr Ambrose giving his blessing to the idea that I may teach reading and writing "to a small group of carefully chosen inmates". The time allowed should be 45 minutes per week, the day and time to be agreed with Alfred Frumley. Slates and slate pencils to be provided by us. I wonder how we will select the students?

Thursday 30th March

The weather has improved.

Mama was unwell this morning with a sick headache and I attended the workhouse meeting on my own. I wanted Theo to accompany me but he declined, saying he had no stomach for the deserving poor and must practise his music. He is such a selfish beast.

I had prepared a list of people I thought suitable for the lessons. These were Rosie, Lizzie Harrold, Tom Bates (Jake's grandfather), a woman named Maggie Coles, a young man, Lenny Shift (always referred to as Shifty), who Rosie had recommended, and a middle-aged man by the name of Ernie Croswell.

Frumley glared at the list and immediately ruled out Ernie. "He's often sick," he said. "It would be a waste of time. And Tom Bates is much too old."

He nominated a man by the name of Ned Wilson instead and said I must make do with five for the first lesson. I was sent into a smaller room, where the rest of the chosen few soon joined me. Shifty is about twenty, ugly, thin as a rake. He suffers with his heart and can hardly breathe but he has a sunny disposition. Ned Wilson is a sullen man who told me he had no time for "stupid book learning" and would rather be breaking up stones and "having a laugh" with the other men. I sent him away and now we are four.

I started them writing straight lines and circles in preparation for the shapes of the alphabet and soon all heads were bent industriously over the slates (which squeaked abominably). After barely 30 minutes Mrs Noye arrived to say the lesson was over. Her smug expression said it all. Of the four, Rosie had done the best work and I feel that her story has taken a turn for the better. The others enjoyed themselves also. Being treated with respect as my "pupils" pleased them greatly. I came home tired but proud of my efforts, with the sound of squeaking slate pencils ringing in my ears!

Friday 31st March

Mrs Pleshey brought us sad news of another workhouse death, and added that there never had been a doctor's visit. We sat for some time discussing what could be done to rid the place of Frumley. The workhouse is grim enough, I thought, without having such an unpleasant workhouse Master.

Mrs Pleshey told us that Frumley has a son who has been in trouble for fighting in the streets after the alehouses have closed at night.

"He's shifty-eyed," she told us, "with dirty black hair to his shoulders and a filthy tongue in his head. Rosie has seen him in the workhouse after dark. She suspects him of stealing from the kitchen."

It was decided that Mrs Pleshey should write to the Commissioners with our suspicions and with a request that Frumley be replaced.

"The letter will be a first step," Mama insisted. "We must not give up until Frumley has been sent away."

Sunday 2nd April

Awoke this morning to heavy rain and a loud banging on the door. Rosie stood there like a drowned rat, with the news that there had been a fire at the workhouse. No one had been hurt, fortunately, but Frumley's office has been damaged. My first thought was that now Frumley has a perfect excuse for the non-appearance of the bills and invoices he professes to have received. Had he started the fire himself?

We invited Rosie into the house and Amy gave her a mug of hot milk and some cake. Mama and I dressed in haste and we all set off back to the workhouse. Leonard Price was already there, surveying the smouldering ruins of the office. Alfred Frumley was poking about in the charred remains of cupboards and shelves. "All gone!" he said mournfully. "All my receipts, bills and invoices. This is a bitter blow!"

Leonard Price rolled his eyes and it was clear *he* didn't believe the fire to have been an accident, either.

I said innocently, "Where were you, Mr Frumley, when the fire took hold?"

Quick as a flash he answered. "I was having supper with some friends. I knew nothing until I was called on by Mrs Noye in a very shaky state, poor soul. The inmates were all turned out in the yard in their nightwear for safety's sake. The women waited to one side while the men helped me put it out. A chain of buckets, that's what we had, and drew our water from the old well." He sounded as though he had rehearsed this little speech.

"And where was your son?" Leonard Price asked. "He lives hereabouts, does he not?"

"He does, yes." Frumley gave him a cunning look. "Lodges right opposite with his wife and child – and another on the way. He saw nothing. Heard nothing."

Mrs Noye appeared and said the inmates were all recovered, had had their breakfast gruel and were back at work. We left them to it and retired to our house, where Leonard Price repeated his suspicions.

"He's covering his tracks," he insisted. "No doubt he had word from the Commissioners that they were going to investigate him and saw a fire as a useful way out. I'm going to oust him from that job if it's the last thing I do!"

Monday 3rd April

Mrs Pleshey came for coffee this morning but I knew the talk would turn to politics and she and

Mama would argue, so I made my excuses and slipped away to write. Mrs Pleshey is a firm supporter of Mr Gladstone, the Prime Minister, but the poor man can do nothing right in Mama's eyes. That is because Papa always voted for the Conservatives and Mr Gladstone is a Liberal. As a modern young woman, I believe women deserve certain rights and should be given the vote. I have read the book by John Stuart Mill entitled *The Subjection of Women*, in which he declares women completely equal with men and demands that we are given the vote. Mama disagrees. She says men are wiser than women and more used to the ways of the world, but she was brought up to think that way and I cannot blame her. My generation is more enlightened. I think also that Mama is so concerned (dare I say "obsessed"?) with the workhouse and its evils that she hardly troubles herself with any other matters. Personally I think Queen Victoria should use her influence to see that women *do* have a say in their own futures and in the running of the country. Sadly I suspect the Queen has so much power as monarch that she doesn't care about the rest of her sisters. (What a thing to say! I shall be locked up in the tower for treason!) But it is true. Last year Lady Amberley spoke up for women, saying that, among other things, girls should have the right to an education as good as that offered to boys. Queen Victoria replied that "women's rights" were a mad, wicked folly and that poor Lady Amberley should be given a good whipping.

Wednesday 5th April

A young constable came to the house to ask about the fire at the workhouse and Mama told him of her suspicions. He has "made a report".

Meanwhile Mrs Pleshey contacted Leonard Price to say she has seen second-hand grey blankets on sale very cheaply in the next town. Has she solved the mystery of the whereabouts of the workhouse's missing blankets?

Thursday 6th April

The writing lesson was delayed by an hour on account of the fire. Frumley is becoming very surly and uncooperative, not to say openly hostile. He obviously knows that the Board of Guardians has lost confidence in him (to put it mildly) and no longer trusts us. I passed his son Tom in town yesterday and he spat in my direction and said something to his companions who laughed aloud and made rude gestures. A lout is the only way to describe Tom Frumley. I shouldn't care to meet him in an alley after dark.

My students made great efforts. We practised A, B, C and D and then each person tried to copy his or her name. I had smuggled in some biscuits which they very much enjoyed. I came away tired but happy that they are making progress.

Mama and I came close to an argument later. She is so eager for the residents of the workhouse to receive an education and yet she seems most determined that I should go no further with mine. I was privately educated at home with Miss Lester (a true martinet) until I was fourteen but now I am of a mind to pick up my education again and take it further. I have suggested to Mama that I apply to Cheltenham Ladies College or the North London Collegiate (for women) but she will not consider it. She insists that I have led a sheltered life and will find it most disagreeable to be "herded with hundreds of other women". I suspect she may fear living alone, but also that she thinks I will turn into "a horrid unwomanly creature" and ruin my chances of finding a husband. Not that I am eager to find one. I want to have some years to myself before I am tied to a husband and family.

I pointed out that finding a husband does not guarantee that a woman will be protected and cared for all her married life. "Remember the case of Caroline Norton, Mama!" I argued. "She lost all her children when her husband took legal proceedings against her. He was even awarded the legacy she had received from her mother as well as all the money she had earned as a writer!"

"She had no need to be earning money!"

"But she wished to write and was good enough to be published."

She frowned at me. "That could not happen again.

Not since the Married Women's Property Act...
Where do you get these ideas from, Edith?"

"I *read*, Mama! Books and newspapers."

She shook her head in despair. Mama can be very irritating but perhaps she is simply afraid of change. Perhaps *her* mother once despaired of *her*! (Will I despair of *my* daughters, if I have any?)

Saturday 8th April

The weather is cool today with heavy clouds. Mama says the workmen are repairing the damaged office. I wonder how much that will cost?

Just after three o'clock a small, wizened man came to our door, sent by Rosie. His name was Harry Horner. He was shabbily dressed but clean. He explained that he needed outdoor relief but Frumley had refused. He had then asked for a few days' indoor relief so that he could regain his strength before moving on, but Frumley suggested that he would not be strong enough for the stone-breaking. It seems he was a watch repairer whose sight has gone due to a cataract in his left eye. He was sacked four months ago and cannot find other employment. He appears a well-spoken man, humiliated to be in this situation. Mama gave him some ham and bread to eat in the garden with a mug of tea while she pondered what best to do. I sat with him out of curiosity to know how people come to this sad condition.

"I had a little room over the shop," he told me sadly. "When I lost the job I lost the roof over my head. I have made my way south to see my cousin who lives in Maidstone but he has moved away."

"Did you have a wife and family?"

His expression darkened. "My Nellie died a few years back, God bless her. She was a good, God-fearing woman but she was taken with the consumption like her mother and aunt before her. We were never blessed with children."

I fetched him another mug of tea. When I went back into the kitchen Mama was wrapping up some cold pork, cheese, an onion and bread for his journey.

She looked up. "I have written him a letter to take with him, saying that I believe him to be an honest craftsman fallen upon hard times. I shall also give him two shillings." Seeing my expression she said, "He may

113

have better luck in Canterbury Workhouse. Not all workhouse Masters are like Frumley. Some have the best interests of the poor at heart." She sighed. "We cannot save everyone, Edith, but we do the best we can."

"Could he not stay in our shed, Mama?"

"And do what, Edith? Do be sensible."

With a heavy heart I watched him stumble away as the first raindrops fell and wondered where he would sleep that night – and how long he would survive.

Tuesday 11th April

Great excitement today. We went round to Mrs Pleshey's house to choose a puppy. I was convinced that nothing would console me for the loss of my darling Prince but Mama knew how much I missed him and persuaded me to take a look at the new litter of Jack Russells. I fell in love with the little creatures (they are eight weeks old now) and chose the smallest one, a little rough-haired bitch with pretty brown and white markings. I shall call her Snip.

Theo had another engagement this evening at a private birthday party. We were not invited but he came home just after eleven o'clock with a broad smile on his face. He had been accompanying members of the family, who sang, and also working in harmony with a violinist and a flautist. They have promised to recommend him. He is now considering whether or not he might develop a partnership with a singer and appear in concert halls as a duo singing popular ballads and light operatic pieces.

Amy's mother has sent a recipe for "Geological Pudding" and Mama says Cook may try it out one day. It consists of alternate layers of chopped figs (with lemon rind and juice) and suet pastry inside a pudding basin. Hence the name (layers of different soil!). I love figs, so cannot wait to taste it.

Thursday 13th April

The weather is so much warmer. I was able to venture out in a tweed jacket and skirt instead of needing a long coat.

More excitement. Alfred Frumley has been taken to the police station for questioning about the fire. If he is put on trial we may have the pleasant task of advertising the post of workhouse Master and interviewing candidates.

In Frumley's absence we heard two applications for outdoor relief and granted both of them – much to Mrs Noye's disgust. One was a woman, Annie Lowe, with a child of two years whose husband has run away with another woman. She earns her living by her mangle and has run into debt. If she cannot pay, she will be thrown out and might then be forced to accept indoor relief, but we granted her the grand sum of seven shillings and she was overcome with gratitude and burst into tears.

The other was Jimmy Corridon, a man of middle years, a carpenter by trade. He was on the road in search of work and had stopped to shelter in a barn during heavy rain. He dozed and awoke to find his tools missing. Without the ability to work he would be forced to casual labouring. There was no denying his agitation and I felt tears pricking at my eyes for his awful predicament. I was glad when we granted him four shillings and sixpence to replace the stolen tools.

Sunday 16th April

Church as usual. I wore the bonnet Theo gave me for my birthday and fancied I looked very fine.

Annie Lowe, the mangle lady, was sitting in the free seats at the back with her little daughter and she smiled at us. I felt like cheering to think we have made someone happy. I prayed earnestly for everyone at the workhouse as well as everyone at home. The vicar was away so we had a visiting preacher who was inclined to dwell on hellfire and brimstone. I thought that many in the workhouse might fancy themselves already in hell.

Theo looked splendid and I saw some of the young women glancing hopefully towards him. Not that their parents would approve of a daughter marrying a musician who scrapes a living on the stage. Thank heavens he isn't an actor.

Yesterday Mama, Mrs Pleshey and I walked together to the next town (Lower Bedbury) and found the man selling the workhouse blankets in the market. He told us that a stranger had offered them to him very cheaply, claiming they had been purchased for a hospital but somewhere the order had been duplicated. So the blankets were "spares".

"I did think it strange," he said, "but they were such a bargain. A Mr Garner. That was his name." He frowned. "Nothing awry, is there, ladies?"

Mrs Pleshey told him the problem and asked him to describe Mr Garner. As expected, his description matched our own Alfred Frumley.

The poor man was flabbergasted but agreed to go with Mrs Pleshey to the nearest constabulary.

Cook made the Geological Pudding for dinner and it was delicious. I shall copy it down into my book of household recipes.

Monday 17th April

Rosie came round today by special invitation. Mrs Noye wanted to refuse permission but didn't dare – she is certainly more biddable without Frumley. Maybe at heart she is a nicer woman but has been corrupted by his influence.

Rosie had a bath and washed her hair, which has started to grow back and is now a riot of short curls. How I envy her. We played with Snip in the garden and then sang with Theo. Rosie knows all the music-hall songs (some are rather naughty!) and a good many ballads. Her great ambition is to visit a London music hall and I would love to go with her, but Mama is quite adamant that respectable people do not attend such places. Rosie has a pleasant voice but she is quite untrained. Theo now sees himself as an expert and did his best to improve her singing. It seems she breathes in the wrong places and slides from one note to the next. Or so he says.

"Make a crisp move from note to note," he told her.

He then tried to make her practise a few scales but she at once lost interest and declared singing "a game for fools"! She cannot concentrate for long and is full of impatience.

But as Theo said later, "She does clean up a treat!"

Mama has made her a petticoat with a lace frill and Rosie has fallen in love with it. She has never had a new garment in all her life. It's to be hoped she manages to keep it. Mama, fearful of Jake's influence, made her promise she will not pawn it.

"If I discover you have parted with the petticoat for any reason, I shall be very angry," Mama told her.

I wonder. It will probably be sold and the money handed to Jake to put towards the non-existent "mangle money". It seems a hard way to earn a living but Rosie is set on it.

Wednesday 19th April

Bad news. Rosie has disappeared. Mrs Noye sent a message soon after eight this morning and we made haste to the workhouse. It seems she went to bed as usual on Tuesday night but was gone by the time the inmates were woken this morning. Mrs Noye finally admitted that there had been a quarrel the previous day over the new petticoat. Rosie was refused permission to wear it for fear of arousing envy in the other women. Rosie lost her temper and punched Mrs Noye, who then slapped and shook her. Rosie was locked in the dormitory for the rest of the day and thus missed the evening meal.

Perhaps Rosie has gone to Jake. Mama was grim-faced by the time we left the workhouse. But no one knows where he lives or even if he has a place to lodge. He may be one of hundreds of men who sleep in a casual ward when the money is there and in doorways when it is absent.

"Maybe Rosie will come to us," I suggested.

Mama sighed. "We can only pray."

Mama, Theo and I spent much of the day walking the streets in search of her, but without success. On reflection, the petticoat may have been a mistake.

Little Snip is also in disgrace! While we were out she chewed a hole in one of Theo's beautiful Italian shoes and he is furious. He gave her a good slap in spite of my entreaties. How does a puppy know what is and isn't a suitable thing to chew? I am not on speaking terms with Theo now and he says that will be a relief.

"You chatter like a starling, Edith, and say nothing worth a brass farthing!"

I hate the boy.

Friday 21st April

A terrible shock. Mama and I were shopping in the High Street when we saw a girl begging. She was holding out her hand to the passers-by. Some people gave her money but others refused and these she miscalled with a few curses, which I cannot write here. She had a shawl over her head and it was some moments before we recognized the voice. It was Rosie!

Without thinking, Mama called out to her and she immediately took to her heels and was last seen disappearing into Bank Street. We walked quickly after her.

"Don't you dare run, Edith!" Mama hissed, ever anxious that I should behave in a ladylike way. There was no sign of Rosie.

I asked Mama about the workhouse rules. Would Rosie be able to return now that she had run off? Mama thought it possible. But would she want to return? She is having a taste of freedom and it may appeal to her. Being homeless means hardships, but being in the workhouse is a horrible alternative.

Sunday 23rd April

A beautiful day. Spring has finally arrived. Theo and I are friends again. He has promised not to chastise Snip in future. If the puppy needs punishing he will tell me and I will see to it. (That way I need only give her a light tap!) Now the weather is better I can train her to sleep in the kennel in the garden. Prince did that until he became too ill and frail.

Rosie has been returned to the workhouse by Jake, of all people! So much for the love he felt for her! Probably found her a nuisance. So now she is in disgrace at the workhouse and no doubt bitterly hurt by Jake's betrayal. Poor Rosie. She seems to stagger through life hurtling from one disaster to the next. How can she ever fit into society with her wild ways and rebellious temperament? At least her story is never dull.

Thursday 27th April

Great excitement. Yesterday evening we went to a concert at the Grand Theatre and watched Theo and a lady called Myra Levant on stage together. First they sang a duet – a sad ballad – while Theo played the piano, and then she sang two solos, which Theo accompanied. The names of the songs escape me but they were not familiar. Mama confided later that she thought the entire programme lacked elegance. In fact she used the word "lowbrow" and I could tell she was disappointed. I pointed out that at least Theo was earning his keep after many years of idling his time away. She had to agree with me on that point.

Myra Levant is not her real name. Theo says she has been on the stage since she was seven and used to be a dancer. Now she is a little too heavy (his word) and has taken to singing instead. I thought she was about 40 but Theo insists 30 is nearer the mark. Rosie would have enjoyed the performance. There were monologues and dances. Also a magician (not a very good one!) and a comedian.

Friday 28th April

Still sunny and bright. Played with Snip in the garden. Theo is learning two more songs – this time from the music halls. I must say, he is taking his work seriously. Wonders will never cease.

Copied two more recipes into my household book – one for a minty toothpaste and another for a soothing balm for burns.

Saturday 29th April

Frumley has been charged with the theft of the blankets and is being held in a prison cell until he goes before the magistrate. I cannot feel any sympathy for the man. He is guilty of that theft and other crimes. Now perhaps the Commissioners will see fit to get rid of him.

Leonard Price is pleased but also nervous of what might follow. He says Tom Frumley has been making threats against all of us, so we have to be careful. I feel more than nervous. I feel afraid. The man is a thug. Mama says it is the price we have to pay for doing what we know is right. Theo simply laughed when I told him. He thinks we are making a mountain out of a molehill and actually called me a silly duffer. I retaliated by saying that anyone who earns a living by singing cheap songs and tinkling a piano has no right to miscall others!

Sunday 30th April

It is half-past six in the morning and I was awoken by a thunderstorm. Rain is pouring down outside and poor little Snip was very frightened and barking at the thunder. Now she is on my bed, whimpering at the lightning and huddled against me for comfort. How can you explain a thunderstorm to an animal?

I am looking forward to the next writing lesson at

the workhouse. My students are making some progress in their learning, but Shifty was missing from the lesson last week. His heart trouble had flared up and he was in the infirmary. This is a room where the sick go when they are too ill to take their place in the normal routine. If necessary they are treated by a doctor, but these visits are rare. It is a question of funds. Mama says there is never enough money allotted and the workhouse Master has to make it last for the year and account for every penny.

Now that Cook knows she will never have to enter the workhouse she feels free to give us her views on the thorny subject.

"If folk in the workhouse are too well off 'tis hardly fair on the rest of us as works hard to keep body and soul together," she told us earnestly. "Not that I'd set foot in the place. Wild horses wouldn't drag me there – but it isn't right!"

I looked at Mama. She said, "But, Cook, we are simply trying to help those who do not *choose* to be destitute. If it were not for the charity of people like us the poor souls would fare much worse than they do."

I thought about Rosie. How could anyone suggest that she would choose to stay there…? But then, when offered a job in the past, she has behaved badly, knowing that she will be sent back to the workhouse. I wish I understood her better.

Evening

The thunderstorm has passed. The rain has washed the streets clean and the air feels fresher. We attended evensong and met Mrs Pleshey with her niece – a very pleasant girl of my age. She and I talked for a while but her conversation was all about young men and I was soon bored. She asked me about my own matrimonial prospects and I said I had none, nor wanted any, at this time.

Tuesday 2nd May

Mama received her copy of the monthly records from the workhouse today and they make interesting reading:

Absconded – 1
Dead – 1
Sent out to domestic service – 2
Given out-relief – 34
Sent to another institution – 3
Still in the workhouse – 107

Which means we now have places for thirteen new applicants because we have 120 beds. I hope the girls sent out to domestic service can hold on to their jobs. Presumably they will live in their place of employment.

The one who absconded was a man named Jack Elliott who has been an inmate on two previous occasions and absconded both times. This time he stayed for ten days before disappearing again. Now he will never be readmitted. It seems that he is a frail man and unused to heavy work. He refuses to do his share of the stone-breaking, saying he is not able-bodied and it would kill him.

He *is* a very small, slight man – somewhat of a weakling – but who is to decide whether a man is able?

The three inmates who were sent elsewhere were a family – a mother and two children who were given the fares back to London where they originally lived. They will then have to reapply to one of the London workhouses.

Wednesday 3rd May

This morning I saw the workhouse women taking their outdoor exercise. There is a large area of badly worn grass to one side of the building, with a wide stone path around it for wet weather when the grass is too muddy, or there is snow on the ground. Such a dreary place. The area is bordered by a high wall on two sides and the other two sides are formed by the L-shaped building itself. The women have two periods a day when they come outside for fresh air and exercise. This sounds quite acceptable but in fact all they do is wander around aimlessly. There are no trees and no flowers nor any seats in which the weak or weary might rest. Nowhere suitable for the children to play when they come out.

Mrs Noye is always on duty and on the lookout for bad behaviour. A few of the women I saw spent their time gazing up at the locked windows of the men's day room where their husbands waved handkerchiefs and mouthed greetings. I confess I was near to tears at this sad sight. It seems desperately unkind to separate husbands and wives for so much of the day and night, but that is the policy. Mama says they do see each other at mealtimes when everyone eats together (except the younger children who have a table in their dormitory and a slightly different diet). The men and women do sit separately for meals but the married couples can at least see each other and exchange greetings. No talking is allowed.

During the outside exercise one of the women stumbled and fell. Rosie and I lifted her on to her feet. She stared round her with a vacuous smile on her face and I realized with a jolt that she was feebleminded. A little blood trickled from the corner of her mouth and she touched it with her finger, then held it up for all to see. "Look?" she murmured.

I took out my handkerchief and offered it to her. She snatched it from me and stared at it, apparently enraptured by the embroidery in the corner. Gently I took it from her and wiped the blood away from the corner of her mouth, but she snatched it back and stared at the bloodstain in horror.

"You've *spoiled* it!" she cried. To my dismay, she burst into clamorous tears, clutching the handkerchief to her chest protectively. Rosie put an arm round the weeping woman and glanced at me reassuringly. "She's probably never 'ad anything pretty. Can she keep it?"

"Certainly."

"I'll go in and wash it for her. She'll get over it."

I watched them go with a lump in my throat and the small crowd that had gathered began to disperse. I wished Mama had been with me, for she understood her "residents" better than I did. I walked back into the building and at the door, I glanced back. A handbell was rung from one of the lower windows. Slowly the women turned towards the sound and began to drift back. I felt somehow shamed by what I had seen. Would I ever truly understand just how empty life could be for the deserving poor?

Thursday 4th May

Discovered at the Board Meeting today that one of the young women to be placed in domestic service is Rosie. A woman has chosen Rosie because her red hair reminds her of her daughter who is dead. Hardly the most sensible reason, but I am pleased that Rosie has been given this opportunity and am crossing my fingers that this time she behaves well.

The doctor was called to Shifty who is very ill with his heart and is still in the infirmary.

Saturday 6th May

Mama went to the workhouse this morning to take some calf's-foot jelly to one of the women who is very sick. Fed a spoonful at a time, it is light and nourishing. I was given permission to visit the children and was surprised to find them sitting on the floor doing very little. They looked so neglected. Hair needed cutting, noses needed wiping. Clothes were faded and seemed to bear no relation to the size of the child. On one boy the trousers were much too big, on another uncomfortably small. The girls wore crumpled pinafores over their dresses and some wore no shoes.

One small girl held a very dirty rag doll to her chest and rocked it to and fro, crooning softly. Another sat watching her with obvious envy. A small boy was piling wooden bricks into a tall stack but each time they reached a certain height they were knocked down by an older boy who seemed to delight in this mean trick. Two little girls sat hand in hand, watching the others with intense concentration, and a boy, perhaps four years old, stood alone in a corner of the room, carefully removing his clothes and folding them into a neat pile.

There was a large toy box, but this seemed to contain very little of use. It held a few tattered books with most of the pages torn out, several dominoes, a coloured ball and a small painted train engine that had lost all its wheels. An elderly resident sat on a chair nearby, watching over the children. She smiled as I approached, stood up and gave a little curtsey.

"I used to be a lady's maid," she told me, "but when she died I came here." She sat down again.

I failed to think of a suitable reply and said instead, "The children have so few toys." She nodded and smiled. I told her that my mother had given the workhouse new toys last Christmas. "Where are they? There was a rocking horse and two dolls, a train set and a game of Snakes and Ladders."

Smiling again, she pointed to a shelf above our heads where all the toys except the rocking horse were on display – still in pristine condition.

"Why aren't they playing with them?" I asked.

She shrugged. "I used to be a lady's maid," she said, "but when she died I came here."

The boy in the corner was now quite naked but after a moment or two he started to dress himself again with meticulous care. I asked about the rocking horse but the poor woman simply stood up, curtsied and sat down again. In desperation I tried to talk to the children but they shrank away, dumb with nervousness. When the tower of bricks fell for the fifth time I could stand it no longer. I reached up and lifted all the new toys down one by one and placed them in front of the children, who stared at them in wonder.

"Play with them!" I cried, but they looked from me to each other and back at me and did nothing.

As I hurried to the door the woman smiled and began to explain that she had once been a lady's maid...

Five minutes later Mrs Noye resented my obvious questions and two spots of angry colour showed in her cheeks. "The toys are kept for high days and holidays," she snapped. "Otherwise they would quickly become worn out. The rocking horse caused so much trouble – every one of them wanted to ride it. We sold it and bought some smaller toys. They have since been broken."

Near to tears, I stammered, "What childhood do they have, these scraps of humanity?"

"They have the satisfaction of knowing that they will not end up stuck in a hot chimney as a sweep's boy!" she cried. "Or sent down a coalmine, or sent hungry into a field for four pence a day to shake a rattle and scare the birds away!" Her chest heaved and her expression unnerved me. "The girls will not be forced to work long hours in a match factory! Do you know what happens to *them*?"

I shook my head.

"The phosphorus gets into their gums and rots their jawbones. It's called phossy jaw!"

"I'm sorry," I whispered. "I didn't think."

She drew a long breath and collected herself. "So … if you'll excuse me, I have work to do!" She turned on her heel and marched away, stiff-backed with righteous indignation.

On the way home Mama listened patiently to my grievances. Then she said sadly, "We do the best we can, Edith. Rome wasn't built in a day."

On a happier note, my portrait progresses and I am becoming rather vain, for I think Mr Flyte flatters me. He makes my eyes bigger and my nose smaller. Theo says he can see no resemblance at all!

Meanwhile I wonder about Rosie. Does her story now have a happy ending? Is she dashing cheerfully about her new home wearing a neat housemaid's uniform? Perhaps she is making friends with the other housemaids… Maybe she is becoming a favourite with her new mistress because of her red hair. Certainly she will be enjoying better food! I shall find out by some means or other. Meanwhile, I am hopeful.

Monday 8th May

Builders are working on the burned-out office at the workhouse so the place is cluttered with planks of wood, bricks, sand, buckets and brushes. Mama suggested that some of the male residents might help with the work, but the idea was turned down most firmly. I suppose the builders want to earn as much as they can from the job and see the workhouse men as cheap competition.

Tuesday 9th May

Great panic in our home this morning in the hour between midnight and one a.m. A small rock was hurled through our front window, smashing the glass and damaging Mama's favourite table – the one left to her by Grandmama when she died. Poor Mama wept when she saw it. Of course we suspect Tom Frumley, but how can we prove it? The crash woke us all and Snip began to bark. I would like to get my hands round Tom Frumley's neck and throttle him. Mama says that is a very unladylike thought – but she would like to do the same! Perhaps we could share the pleasure! What worries me is the feeling that this may only be the beginning.

Wednesday 10th May

The news we all dreaded. Rosie has been sent back to the workhouse as "not suitable for domestic employment". Apparently she was rude to her employer, Herbert Billington, and was described by Mrs Billington as "a wicked little troublemaker". Rosie's version is that Billington "was a sight too free with his hands" and pretended on several occasions to adjust the straps of her apron so that he could fumble her chest. Mrs Noye is furious, but Mama says Rosie is well out of that house because servants are always vulnerable to abuse of that kind.

Mama thinks Theo is becoming rather too fond of Myra Levant. He asked if Myra might come to our house tomorrow for a last-minute rehearsal of the songs they are performing together. Mama said yes, and she and I are very intrigued to see Myra at close hand.

Cheering news. Alfred Frumley will not be returning to his post and it has been readvertised.

Oh yes! Our broken window has been repaired and Mama says we are to put the matter out of our minds and that such a bully must not frighten us.

Thursday 11th May

More trouble at the workhouse. We had a stormy session with Jon Simms, the "porter", who complained that he has been asked to cut the residents' hair. This used to be done by a lowly paid medical attendant "who has left to better himself". Simms has been there for years and earned a little pocket money by manning the front door. He insisted he was *not* going to cut hair! After a long tussle it has been agreed that he *will* do it, but only on payment of a small increase in his (very meagre) wages.

Today's writing lesson went well and I have introduced my pupils to reading by way of cards containing simple words – mat, cat, dog, bog. Rosie is making amazing progress. She can write her name and can already recognize the four words. She has asked me for a book – any book – and Mama suggests a Bible. I will take it with me next week.

Friday 12th May

Myra Levant came, as promised, and after she and Theo had practised a little, Mama and I were invited to listen to their songs. I have to say they are rather good together, though her voice is stronger than Theo's and tends to dominate. But she laughs a lot and Theo is infatuated with her. They have another engagement booked – to sing at a charity concert in the army's drill hall in aid of the Fund for the Relief of Distressed Gentlewomen.

What a dreadful phrase. It refers to respectable middle-class women who have fallen on hard times and now depend on charity if they are to stay out of the workhouse – like Miss Lymme, who lives nearby. She was once a governess to a wealthy family that had seven children. Her home was with the family for 23 years while all the children grew up and were educated by her. Then she was cast out at the age of 59 without a farthing to her name. She lodges now with an elderly widow and pays six pence a night for a small attic room. The poor soul exists on the charity of a second cousin and occasional grants from the Fund for the Distressed Gentlewomen. Without this aid, poor Miss Lymme would be in Stoneleigh Workhouse.

Saturday 13th May

We attended the charity concert held at the drill hall in the town and there was a good audience. Theo says they raised just under 45 guineas in ticket sales. I enjoyed it. Mostly, I confess, for the things that went wrong. The magician's tricks were hopeless (he was an amateur and friend of the organizer!) and the man giving the monologue twice forgot his words and had to be prompted. However, there was a professional acrobat who pulled off astonishing feats and a man and woman who performed a Spanish flamenco dance with wildly clicking castanets, wonderfully swirling skirts and stamping feet.

Theo looked very handsome in his black dress suit and Myra Levant very vivacious in red and black. On stage she looked much younger. I expect it's the stage make-up. They had two spots in the programme and sang music-hall songs – humorous or sad, but nothing bawdy. It reminded me of Rosie at the piano with Theo. If only things had been different I could imagine her up there on stage, her red curls glinting in the footlights.

Why does she behave so badly? Does she want to remain at the workhouse? She is pretty and healthy and quick to learn. Everything is in her favour, but she is like a wild horse that doesn't want to be tamed.

Wednesday 17th May

More trouble. While Mama and I were shopping this morning we met Tom Frumley and she at once accused him of breaking our window.

He denied it. "You're just a meddling old biddy who has it in for my pa!" he insisted. "He's gone to prison for something he didn't do, and you'll live to regret it!" He glared at me. "Keep looking over your shoulder, the pair of you!"

"Is that a threat?" Mama demanded.

"A threat? Never! Would I threaten anyone? It's a bit of friendly advice!"

Mama is pretending not to be bothered by his words but I think she is as frightened as I am. I do wish she had simply ignored him. I thought discretion was the greater part of valour!

Thursday 18th May

We had no sooner arrived for today's meeting than there was a commotion further along the corridor and the door flew open. Rosie came in dragging an older woman by the hand. The woman wore a threadbare nightdress and her greying hair was uncombed. Mrs Noye jumped to her feet at once.

"How dare you force your way in like—"

Mrs Pleshey put out a restraining hand to silence her.

Rosie said, "This woman has just come from the infirmary. She wants to complain."

Mrs Noye was pale. "Lorna Downes is a troublemaker," she stammered.

Mrs Pleshey said, "We'll hear her." She turned to Rosie. "You may go now, Rosie."

"I'm with 'er." Rosie tossed her head defiantly. "Go on Lorna. Tell 'em."

The woman, a timid soul, began to stammer her complaint. "Some of the patients have skin troubles … rashes and the like." She swallowed hard and went on.

"We ... we have to share the towels with them." She looked nervously at each of us and went on. "The doctor never comes to see us and —"

Mama leaned forward. "But there's a nurse."

Rosie snorted. "A nurse? If you mean Liddie Kemp, she's one of us. Claims to 'ave been a midwife but knows next to nothing. And patients in the infirmary are supposed to 'ave a special diet to help them recover their strength, but they only get what the rest of us get."

It was then decided that the Guardians should inspect the infirmary and see for themselves. Not a visit I would wish to repeat. The room, medium-sized, smelled of disinfectant overlaid with sickness, dirt, tainted breath and something I think was probably stale urine (and worse) from stained mattresses which were mercifully hidden from our view. I wondered if bed bugs also were to be found therein and shuddered. The room contained ten beds on which eighteen patients lay in various states of discomfort and disarray. One patient had slid down and was tightly enclosed in the blanket, wrapped like an Egyptian mummy. Another had thrown off the blanket and lay exposed to view in a dirty nightgown. It dawned on me that this was an unscheduled visit and we were seeing the infirmary as it normally was. There had been no time to make hurried improvements in the hope of impressing us.

We walked slowly along the row of beds in shocked silence. The room was bare of any comfort. Another patient, a woman of middle age, was propped up against the iron bed head. Her eyes were closed and I hoped for her sake that she was asleep and enjoying a pleasant dream but I doubted it. Next to her a woman lay tangled in a sheet. Her eyes were wide open but she seemed unaware of our presence, muttering incoherently as though feverish. Under each bed I noticed a chamber pot, many filled to overflowing and badly in need of emptying.

The "nurse" was, as Rosie had said, one of the inmates promoted to the position to save the expense of a trained nurse. She was sitting at the far end of the room knitting, but she hastily stuffed the work down beside her stool when we reached her end of the room. As she stood up, agitated by our sudden appearance, she made a futile effort to tidy her shabby clothes and smooth her worn apron. Throughout the entire visit, which lasted a bare five minutes, nobody spoke.

I was heartily glad to be out of there and closed the door behind us with deep relief. Please, God, I prayed, never let me find myself in such a place. Selfish, I know, but at least I had learned that here was another area of the workhouse that desperately needed attention.

When we were back in the boardroom a heated discussion ensued. Mama insisted that the "nurse" was not to blame. Liddie Kemp was paid a pittance and for that was expected to wash the patients, change the beds, give them their medicine (if there was any) and feed those who were too weak to feed themselves. Mrs Noye confessed that the official nurse had left months ago and no one had notified the Board of Guardians. Another money-saving trick, I thought angrily.

Leonard Price said, "Were the nurse's wages drawn after she left?"

Mrs Noye turned pale. "I … I do not probe too deeply," she stammered. "It was made clear a long time ago that if I asked too many questions I might find myself out of a job."

As we walked home, Mama explained that from time to time legislation is passed in Parliament to try and improve the workhouse system. "Succeeding governments frequently 'forget' the poor because they do not have the vote, but when they *do* pass a law to help them there are always unscrupulous people like Frumley prepared to abuse the system. It is never a priority with the government but there are always concerned groups agitating for change and there *is* progress, but it's woefully slow." She shrugged and fell silent.

I am amazed at Mama's resilience. If I had been engaged in the work as long as she has, I would have given up hope years ago.

Saturday 20th May

Three cheers for Theo and Myra who are now officially a duo! They have received several more bookings. One is to sing for a wealthy family whose son is soon to be 21 years old. It will be held at Thurlow Park – a big house with acres of grounds to the north of Stoneleigh. Theo and Myra will be part of a concert to be held after the evening meal and there will also be a ballet dancer, a clown and a storyteller. It is very well paid and will almost certainly lead to other private engagements.

Poor Mama cannot decide whether to be pleased or sorry that the partnership is thriving. It looks as though Theo and Myra are fond of each other but Mama confided to me that Katherine (who originally adopted Theo) would never have chosen such a woman for him. I asked Theo if Myra has ever been married and he looked surprised and said he has never asked. He is evidently not as worldly-wise as I imagined.

Tuesday 23rd May

A very black day. We were attacked in broad daylight! Mama and I were on the way home from Leonard Price's house when two loutish youths sprang from an alley and knocked us to the ground. My head struck the cobbles and I was dazed, but as I struggled to sit up I saw them kicking Mama. They stole her purse and ran off but a passing man ran after them. A constable was called and one of the louts was caught, but poor Mama was in a terrible state. She was carried home with a painful ankle and various bruises and a deep cut over her left eye.

"It must have been Tom Frumley's doing!" I mumbled, still dizzy from the fall on the cobbles.

Mama agreed. "He's too crafty to do it himself but he may have inspired them – or even *paid* them to do it."

She was still shivering from the pain and shock and went straight to bed. Amy took up sweet tea and Cook made her a lemon custard which she says will be easy to digest. Foolishly I refused to go to bed, but I too was trembling all over. Mrs Pleshey heard of the attack and brought round some beef tea. She spoke so kindly, I burst into tears.

Wednesday 24th May

Mama is not at all well. The pain in her ankle is very bad and she was unable to sleep last night. I have sent for our doctor. Her face is puffy and black and blue and she aches all over. I helped her to wash this morning and she managed to brush her teeth.

Rosie turned up unannounced because she had

heard on the grapevine about the attack. She brought Mama some lilies, which she "found" in a churchyard! I asked her how she manages to escape so often from her "prison".

She grinned. "I climb out the window and shin down the drainpipe."

Rosie says she will ask Jake to find out who attacked Mama. I wish she wouldn't interfere. She always seems to cause more trouble though she doesn't intend it. Her hair was very dirty and to my surprise she asked if she could wash it here before returning to the workhouse. I willingly gave her some hot water, soap and a towel and left her in the outhouse.

When the doctor came, he thought Mama's ankle might also be broken so she must now have it properly examined and treated.

Saturday 27th May

I think the doctor is worried. He says the wound in Mama's ankle may be infected. The ankle *is* broken and continues to hurt, but Mama has been given something to lessen the pain.

Went to the Board Meeting alone on Thursday so that I could report back to Mama. The Local Government Board has advertised for a new workhouse Master and this morning we interviewed three local people for the job of infirmary nurse. It was agreed Stoneleigh should offer the newly recommended rate of £20 annually "all found" – which means board and lodgings free. (A great improvement on the last nurse who received only £12. Little wonder that she didn't stay long.)

One of the applicants had trained in London for eleven months at St Thomas's Hospital. The second was very enthusiastic but had no training at all. The third had acted as an untrained midwife when she was younger (but Mrs Noye smelled alcohol on her breath). They appointed the first, whose name is Ellen Carey, and have resolved to keep a watchful eye on her progress and on the infirmary.

On Friday I was invited to attend the workhouse at eight o'clock in the morning to see how the men are organized into working parties for the day. Allotting the chores was Frumley's job, but in his absence Mrs Noye was undertaking it. The men gathered in a sullen group in their main room and she read out the following:

Albert Hines, Donald Twiss, Fred Burbage, Allan Carter and Steven Baggs – stone-breaking.

Edward Norris and James Ord – lavatories.

Bert Mills and Jed Simmons – shifting coal from the outside store to the boiler room.

Simon Denton – stoking the boiler.

Larry Scott – cleaning the windows on the ground floor.

I was free to inspect the work but soon realized that the men resented my presence and I could not blame them. The lavatories were in a disgusting state and smelled so abominable that I wondered when they had last been cleaned. The long wooden seat (with "privy holes" at intervals) had to be scrubbed and the buckets emptied somewhere (I chose not to investigate further!) and the floors mopped with soapy water. One man deliberately flicked filthy water in my direction and I hastily withdrew, followed by the harsh sounds of their laughter.

The huge man who shifted coke for the boiler, Simon Denton, seemed to love his job and went to it with a furious energy, hurling shovelfuls of coke into the enormous boiler at great speed and humming tunelessly throughout. Could he possibly be enjoying it? I eventually discovered he would do no other work, nor would he stop except to eat and go to bed.

By way of contrast, the man sent to wash the windows moved at a snail's pace, assuring me that he suffered from a disease which had foxed the doctors for years. This disease showed itself, he told me, in a great lethargy of mind and body. I did not believe a word of it – but who am I to judge? Perhaps this is his way of making life in the workhouse almost tolerable.

Edward Bush, one of the older men, told me about "bone-crushing" which has now fortunately been banned. In years past bones were collected weekly from neighbouring butchers and slaughter houses, and these were pounded and crushed by hand to be sold as fertilizer. In a small room each man sat on a wooden stool placed around a trough of broken bones. To crush the bones each man used a heavy metal tool called a rammer which weighed 28 pounds. The smell of decayed gristle and bone must have been overpowering.

Bush looked at me slyly. "We found human bones once," he whispered.

His neighbour, Raymond Taggart, nodded vigorously. "*Human* bones."

I stared at them, unable to believe what he was saying. "You mean ... someone had been *murdered*?"

Bush nodded.

I swallowed nervously. "How did you know the bones were human?"

He gave a scornful laugh. "Course they were. I mean, a human skull looks nothing like a cow's skull. And there were leg bones and a hand—"

"Stop!" I leaned back against the wall, my legs weak, as the horrid vision floated before me.

Bush giggled. "Never told no one."

Taggart shook his head. "'Cept you, Miss."

Bush giggled again and rolled his eyes.

I tried not to show my horror. "What ... what happened to the bones?"

"Crushed 'em in with the rest. Why not? They was dead." He put a finger to his lips and grinned.

Bush nodded, his expression solemn. I looked at him wondering whether or not to believe him yet something about the way it was told made me think it was the truth.

"You told *no one*?"

Bush tapped his nose. "Not my business, was it. Why should I help them buggers?"

The coarse word had slipped out. Taggart nudged

156

him and Bush said, "Oh! Begging your pardon, Miss?"

I was thinking of what he'd done. He'd covered up a crime. Maybe he is now an accessory to a crime, but I saw his reasoning at once and felt a kind of sympathy. It was a way to revenge himself against authority. It had given him a sensation of power to deliberately withhold important information. I fled the room with my stomach heaving and went home. I shall say nothing. The evidence is gone, so the police could do little. I hope this does not make me an accomplice.

The shock remains, however, and from time to time I shudder at the knowledge that the murderer is probably still out there somewhere. I wonder if Queen Victoria has any notion of the depths of depravity to which some of her subjects sink, and what a huge gulf there is between the few rich and millions of poor? If this were France we should no doubt have a revolution as they did at the end of the last century and tumbrels would rumble in the streets of London. What a fearsome thought!

Two years ago one of the inmates at Stoneleigh hanged himself from a ceiling beam in the dining hall, and I am beginning to understand why.

Sunday 28th May

Theo and I went to church twice today, to pray most earnestly for a change in Mama's condition. I also asked God to help Theo with his career and to watch over Snip who has so many ways of getting out on to the street and will, I fear, end up under the hooves of a passing dray horse. After the morning sermon we sang "Abide with me" which used to be one of my favourite hymns but now it reminds me of the unfortunates in the workhouse. When we sang, "Help of the helpless, O abide with me," my eyes filled with unexpected tears.

Monday 29th May

A shock for Theo. It seems Myra Levant has a husband and four children! The husband turned up here yesterday while they were rehearsing a new song and there was a noisy confrontation between husband and wife. I kept out of the way but enquired later.

"Hector left her two years ago and she thought he'd gone for good," Theo told me. "There was another woman involved." He sighed. "When he finally came back to her she found herself unable to forgive him and *she* left *him*, and the children, and went back to her profession on the stage."

"But why has Hector suddenly reappeared?"

"He's only just found out where she is and is begging for a second chance."

It seems the couple are now properly reconciled and Myra is returning to her husband and children. Poor Theo will have no partner for his music engagements – and the important birthday-party booking is only a week away.

"I have an idea," I told him. "Why don't you sing with Rosie?"

"Rosie Chubb? Are you mad, Edith?"

"She looks very pretty when she's cleaned up and she knows all the songs. Her hair is still quite short but she can wear a bonnet. You have time to rehearse. The workhouse cannot complain because it will be paid employment."

I finally persuaded him it might be a good idea. Certainly better than cancelling an important engagement. He will come with me tomorrow to see if Rosie is interested.

I am anxious about Mama. She is getting worse. She has a high temperature and the doctor thinks the infection in her ankle has now led to poisoning of the blood. Mama seems to be half-asleep all the time and very vague.

Tuesday 30th May

Rosie was thrilled at the prospect of singing with Theo and not at all nervous about going on stage. She will come each afternoon for two hours to rehearse with Theo, and I will alter one of my dresses to fit her by taking up the hem. I'll add some bright artificial flowers to give the dress a bit of colour and make it look more theatrical. Rosie will need some better shoes, of course, and I will lend her my best beads… No. On second thoughts, I will buy her some cheap glass beads, which she can keep. I don't want my jewellery to end up in Jake's hands or in the pawnshop!

Mrs Noye seemed rather excited by Rosie's prospects, much to my surprise. Maybe there is a nicer woman hidden inside the unpleasant one. If so, deprived of Frumley's evil influence, she might well blossom.

Also spoke to Ellen Carey, the new nurse at the workhouse. She seems a kind-hearted woman. She is keeping on Liddie Kemp as an assistant and will attempt to pass on to her some basic nursing skills. The infirmary looked much cleaner and one of the patients confided that they will each have a cup of milk with their breakfast *and an egg twice a week for their tea!*

They were pathetically excited about these small improvements.

Friday 2nd June

This morning I looked at Mama as she lay sleeping and resisted the urge to waken her. I reminded myself that bed rest is very valuable and that while we sleep the body heals itself. "It will take time," I muttered.

Why don't the medical men invent something that will cure these dread infections that occur inside the body? It is said that during the war in the Crimea more soldiers died from infections and diseases than from the wounds themselves.

Mama looked very flushed and the doctor has described her condition as "still very troublesome". I fetched some refreshing lavender water and left it on her bedside table with some clean handkerchiefs.

Sunday 4th June

Theo went with me to church this morning and we prayed for Mama to recover soon. I also prayed for all the inmates of the workhouse and the staff.

The sun shone in through the stained-glass window and I felt at peace with the world. It reminded me that there is a small chapel in the workhouse and presumably a chaplain though I have never met him. I will make it my duty to enquire about the services. Have they, too, been neglected? I do think it would help the residents to spend a tranquil hour in the chapel on Sunday mornings. Depending on the quality of the sermons, of course!

Monday 5th June

The portrait is finished at last. Mr Flyte has made me look very beautiful. I look at least nineteen and very elegant, with lustrous eyes and hair like silk. Mama will be delighted when she sees it.

Mrs Pleshey called on me today to tell me of an incident at the workhouse, which has delighted her. "It concerns baby Billy," she said. "When his mother died, it seemed young Billy was doomed to stay in the workhouse but suddenly his luck has changed." Mrs Pleshey's face shone with excitement. She explained that the workhouse had received a letter from a childless woman of some means who wished to adopt one of the orphans. On being offered young Billy, she at once accepted.

"It only remains for the paperwork to be done," she told me. "Her husband is a senior clerk on the railway and they can provide a good home for him. Can you imagine the difference this makes to his fortunes! He will grow up in a loving family and free from want. We must thank God for such a miracle!"

Delighted, we celebrated with a small glass of sherry. It is so rare, I thought happily, that we have really *good* news like this.

Tuesday 6th June

A miserable day. I have spent most of it resting in my room with a bad headache. I tried to lose myself in Charlotte Brontë's *Jane Eyre* (the story of a governess who marries her employer) but the small print strained my eyes so I gave up. Mama loves the story – and so does Queen Victoria, apparently. She described it some years ago as "powerfully and admirably written". (Such praise from a royal personage!) What a shame that more governesses cannot marry their wealthy employers instead of being cast into the workhouse when they have outlived their usefulness.

Cook sent up some asparagus soup, which was very soothing, and sent me gently into a pleasant afternoon sleep. Cook thinks I have overtired myself and that may be so. Without Mama I have been helping in the kitchen. I had never realized how much time Cook spends on her feet. It made my back ache.

Theo took it into his head to take Snip for a walk but found her "unresponsive and a handful". At supper he offered to devise a training programme for her but I refuse to allow it. Snip is *my* dog.

I said, "If you must train something, train Rosie Chubb. She truly *is* a handful!"

He laughed so much he nearly choked.

Wednesday 7th June

A terrible afternoon. The doctor tries constantly to reassure me but he has finally expressed doubts about Mama's leg, which may never be as good as new.

"You mean she will not be able to walk?" I cried in horror.

He pursed his lips. "If she recovers, she—"

"If?" I stared at him.

My accusing tone put him at once on the defensive. "Miss Lorrimer, you have to understand that bed rest is the best we can offer her and only time will tell. One day perhaps the scientists will discover new cures – pills or medicines, even drugs that will fight infections. Maybe in ten years, maybe 50 years, who knows. *If* your mother recovers she will almost certainly walk with a limp."

I sat down suddenly on a nearby chair and tried not to cry at this dreadful prognosis.

He said that I should pray for her and added, "God moves in mysterious ways."

Effectively silenced by his angry words, I watched him go. Yes, I would pray for Mama but God's ways must be very mysterious indeed, I thought. All the inhabitants of the workhouse must pray to be elsewhere but their sad little prayers go unanswered. However, I called in at the church and lit a candle for Mama.

Thursday 8th June

The Board met as usual and a letter was read out by Leonard Price. A new workhouse Master, approved by both the Board of Guardians and the Local Goverment Board, will arrive within the next few days. Please God he is better than the last one. His name is Edward Phipps and he is 46 years old. He worked as a police constable when younger and was an assistant to a workhouse Master in Exeter for three years, but retired through ill health. He is now recovered, his wife is dead and he wishes to resume work. He was the only applicant. It seems that poor pay and unhappy conditions do not make the role of workhouse Master very attractive.

An explanation was given by Mrs Noye as to why three men who applied for overnight stay in the casual ward last night were refused admission. Apparently they were all very drunk and quarrelsome, and Mrs Noye says she was fearful for her safety and the safety of the other inmates. She sent for a constable and they were taken away to sober up in a cell overnight.

After what happened a week ago I applaud her prompt action.

After the meeting I talked with the chaplain who is a small, timid man, young but prematurely grey. He told me that all the fit inmates are expected to attend the Sunday service, which lasts for an hour. He confessed that many of them sleep through the service but he turns a blind eye.

I tried to imagine the scene – heads lolling forward, a few snores and grunts. "Is there music?" I asked. "For the hymns and psalms."

"No, and many of the inmates cannot read, so the hymnals are of very little use."

He also gives comfort to the dying and offers help at all times but is rarely approached. "The long-term inmates accept their fate and don't expect to better themselves." he explained.

I suggested a short prayer meeting mid-week.

He shrugged. "They have to work the set hours 'in useful labour' to earn the food they eat. If you wish, we could discuss the idea with the new Master when he comes."

I came away seriously discouraged. Perhaps I should confine my efforts to improving the residents' physical condition and leave their spiritual welfare to the chaplain.

Friday 9th June

A year ago today Charles Dickens died. He was only 58 but they said he had been overworking for a long time, giving his famous readings. He was such a well-loved author and known all over the world. Will anyone ever take his place, I wonder?

Saturday 10th June

Theo and Rosie are practising their music. (She does have a sweet voice.)

Today the doctor told me there was little change in Mama's condition. Please God return Mama to me in full health and I will *never,* NEVER complain about anything again.

After Rosie had returned to the workhouse we awaited the arrival of Francis Flyte and the finished portrait, which is now framed. Of course Theo pretended not to recognize me and insists that Francis Flyte needs spectacles to improve his eyesight.

Monday 12th June

I am so frightened. Poor Mama is in a critical condition. Yesterday the workhouse chaplain said a prayer for her during the service. I hope God is listening. Mrs Pleshey brought some calf's-foot jelly for me to give to Mama. I did not have the heart to tell her Mama is unable to take any food and that even water has to be trickled into her mouth with a spoon.

Wednesday 14th June

Message from the workhouse to say Edward Phipps has arrived and has moved his belongings into his private rooms on the first floor. He *must* be an improvement on Alfred Frumley.

The workhouse chaplain will ask the new Master tomorrow whether a short prayer meeting every Wednesday evening might be offered after the evening meal. No sermon and no hymns, but prayers and possibly an informal discussion with regard to spiritual needs. I shall keep my fingers crossed that Mr Phipps agrees at least to a trial period.

Thursday 15th June

Rosie is beginning to behave a *little* better now that she is spending more time at a private home instead of the workhouse. The hours she spends with Theo must be having a calming effect on her. Having said that, a silver candle snuffer did go missing but as soon as I mentioned it, it was mysteriously returned to its place on the sideboard. Perhaps Rosie is also beginning to understand the difference between right and wrong. I can hardly wait to see her on stage with Theo. I think she will look the part, but will she develop stage fright?

Theo and I took Rosie to church with us yesterday to pray for Mama. She was rather an embarrassment, as she could see no point in whispering and was a great fidget – rushing about to inspect the flower arrangements, opening several hymnals (perhaps she did not realize they were all the same), examining the hassocks and wanting to light the altar candles. Rather like an overexcited child, I thought. There was no service in progress, but a few people were kneeling at prayer and began to mutter about her behaviour. After a few minutes we gave up and we took her out again. I cannot blame her. Life in the workhouse has not prepared her for the real world. Sadly, I suspect the cards are stacked against her.

The Board Meeting this morning was not without incident. Edward Phipps seems very cooperative. (Time will tell!) A Mrs Stride arrived, begging for shelter for herself and her eleven-year-old son, Amos. She was thin as a rake and very pale, with signs of advanced consumption. Amos is tall for his age, with regular features, a good complexion, corn-coloured hair and dark brown eyes. (I think that one day he will be handsome.) He didn't speak but glared round him with a look of great resentment, as though we were to blame for their troubles. He clutched a kettle, a bundle of what looked like clothing and two saucepans. Mrs Stride held a rolled-up blanket, a stool and a small bundle of cutlery.

It seems the family were living in a tied cottage while the husband worked on the farm doing maintenance. His wife worked long hours topping and tailing turnips in all weathers and doing other work in the fields while the boy did what he could, feeding the horses, chopping firewood, running errands and the like. Every extra penny counted in that little household.

Two weeks ago her husband was killed in a fall from a barn roof and Mrs Stride and the boy were evicted from their farm cottage because it would be needed for the family of the labourer who replaced the dead man. A week after the funeral the landlord had their meagre possessions dumped in the lane while all the neighbours watched the eviction.

"Not that we had much," Mrs Stride told us, her voice heavy with misery. "Three stools, a chest for our clothes, a couple of mattresses, pots and pans – and the clothes we stood up in. Oh yes! And a blanket and two pillows stuffed with straw. Everything else had already gone to the pawnshop! It was raining hard so everything was soon sodden…" Distressed by the memory, poor Mrs Stride broke down in tears and young Amos put his arm round her shoulders, his expression grim.

They had no money to hire any kind of transport so the woman and her child had to leave everything except what they could carry. She and Amos are walking the 40 miles to her parents' home. It is obvious they are both suffering from malnutrition. Mr Phipps granted indoor relief for a few days in the infirmary in the hope that Mrs Stride can regain her strength. Poor soul. How desperately easy it is for hard-working people to lose everything and find themselves utterly dependent on charity.

Friday 16th June

Another blow this morning. The doctor has now warned us that even if Mama survives, the persistent infection *may* have damaged her brain. Thank heavens I am not married or about to marry. I shall be able to nurse Mama. She *must* survive.

Tomorrow is Theo's singing engagement. Rosie looks wonderful in the dress and bonnet. Theo bought her a pair of pretty buttoned boots. I'd give anything to be there but it's out of the question as it is a private affair.

Saturday 17th June

Mrs Pleshey came by this morning soon after nine o'clock to ask me to accompany her to the workhouse, as there was an urgent problem. When we arrived Mr Phipps was striding up and down his office looking deeply troubled, and Mrs Noye was wringing her hands in great agitation. Young Amos Stride has disappeared and his mother is hysterical with fear and shock. I asked that she be given some hot milk with a spoonful of sugar or honey and Mr Phipps agreed. While Mrs Pleshey talked with Mr Phipps I tried to calm the poor mother who, sipping the hot milk, was blaming herself for not "keeping an eye" on the boy. It seems he ran off during the night while everyone was asleep. We shall have to notify the police who will look out for him. His mother thinks he will try to find work.

"Amos knows how ashamed I am to be here," she told me. "His father always said he would borrow a shotgun and kill us all rather than let us end up in such a place – and here we are!" Her eyes filled again with tears.

"But you are only passing through," I told her. "Things will be better when you reach your parents."

She shrugged. "My parents are living in one room above a stable block. Pa mucks out the horses and Ma does a bit of washing for the owners. We cannot stay there for long, but I didn't know what else to do."

In other words, I thought sadly, they might well end up as permanent residents in yet another workhouse.

Much later we had some *good* news. Mama has "turned the corner" and her temperature is dropping.

She was asleep when I went up to see her but the doctor was more cheerful about her prospects.

I am too tired to wait up for Theo so I will have to hear about how the engagement went in the morning.

Sunday 18th June

At church this morning a prayer of thanks was given for Mama's recovery. Now I shall have to keep my part of my bargain with God and never complain!

Theo tells me he and Rosie were a resounding success! So something else is going well. What have I done to deserve such good fortune? Theo and Rosie had to sing two encores, they were *so* popular and Theo has a further booking for the last week in June. He brought Rosie back here to change her clothes and gave her a shilling before escorting her back to the workhouse. He says she went back "happy as a lark", delighted with her adventure.

Mama has eaten some milk jelly and is taking liquids normally again. I wanted to hug her for coming through such a lengthy ordeal but she looks very fragile. (I settled for a kiss instead.) Theo told her about Rosie and the singing, and she smiled. She seems to understand what we say but the doctor said it will take her a little time to reach full health. Mama may be a semi-invalid for the rest of her life, but at least she is alive. I wonder, would Mama have survived in the workhouse infirmary? The answer is a resounding NO!

Mr Phipps has given his approval to the chaplain's request for a prayer meeting and they are to test the idea for six weeks. He seems a genuinely well-intentioned man and will make an excellent Master. I took a few books and toys for the children and he promised to see that they are in constant use along with the others on the high shelf!

Monday 19th June

A sad start to the morning. Myra Levant came to the house to say her farewells to Theo. She is returning to London with her husband and children. Theo was very upset and at first refused to speak with her but Myra has apologized to him for her deception and they finally parted somewhat tearfully.

Amos Stride is found! A constable saw him trying to climb through the window of a house. He was taken back to the workhouse to be positively identified and I was notified. (Mrs Pleshey was not available and Mr Price is in bed with a bad back.) I hurried round, determined if possible to prevent young Amos from being charged with a crime. The last thing Mrs Stride needs is to have her only son arrested.

At the workhouse the constable insisted that the boy was breaking and entering and it is a punishable offence. Amos looked sullen and his mother began stammering a defence. My heart sank.

"But the boy did not actually do any damage, nor did he steal anything," I argued.

The workhouse Master was quick to support my claim. "Nor did he enter the house."

The constable scowled. "Only because I stopped him."

"You *prevented* the crime," I agreed. "Well done, Constable."

He seemed unsure how to react to this unexpected praise but Mrs Stride gave me a quick glance and I saw a glimmer of hope in her eyes.

The constable hesitated. He looked at Amos. "What were you going to steal, eh? What were you after?"

The boy found his voice. "Something proper to eat – for me and Ma. Not the horrible pap they give us in this place! Pa used to say that—"

"Amos!" cried his mother, one hand fearfully pressed to her chest. "Don't speak to the constable like that!" She looked at the constable. "We brought him up to show respect to the law. He's never done anything like this before. *Never*! I swear it on God's name!"

I held my breath. After some further argument, in which Edward Phipps again spoke up for the boy, the constable agreed that no real harm had been done and no actual crime committed. He left after a stern warning to Amos that he should stay on the straight and narrow in future.

As I returned home I thought how near Amos Stride had been to disaster. He might have been sent to a reformatory where he would have mixed with more hardened offenders, would certainly have learned many bad habits and almost certainly lost all respect for authority. At least he has been given a second chance. Perhaps when he and his mother reach his grandparents a little work might be found for Amos in the stables. No matter how poorly paid, the work would keep him out of mischief. I try to console myself with this thought.

Thursday 22nd June

Mama's condition is much better. She has lost weight but she can still smile. Cook promises to "feed her up" in the coming weeks. Mama sleeps most of the time and when she does wake, she finds it tiring to talk, but there is plenty of time.

Theo and I have had a talk about Rosie. I feel she should be given a chance to make good in the outside world, away from the restraints of the workhouse. I have suggested that we find her a small room somewhere nearby and allow her to pay the rent from what she earns singing with Theo. It is a big risk. Theo thinks she will abscond, taking the money and my clothes with her.

"We shall most likely never set eyes on her again," he warned.

I confided in Mrs Pleshey, to see if she had any ideas

or knew of a small, cheap room to let. To my great delight she did. Tomorrow I shall take Rosie to see the room but already I begin to see problems. Rosie has never learned to cook. How will she feed herself? Will she keep the room clean? Will she wash and iron her clothes? Most important of all, will she fit in or will her outrageous behaviour mean that she is thrown out within a week? We shall see.

Friday 23rd June

The room is in an attic in a house down by the river. The landlady is Mrs Defoe; a plump, kindly woman, but very talkative. Rosie, to my surprise, insists she will be lonely. After the workhouse I should have expected her to look forward to being alone. Not so. Rosie seems genuinely nervous but reluctantly agreed to "give it a go".

Mrs Defoe has suggested that she cook for her lodger twice a day — porridge for breakfast and a midday meal — and that Rosie fends for herself the rest of the time. (Fruit and maybe a bit of bread and cheese or ham. Simple to buy and prepare and not expensive.) In return for the meals, Rosie must help Mrs Defoe with the washing and ironing and some housework.

Tomorrow night she and Theo have another musical engagement. She will move into her new room on Sunday.

Saturday 24th June

Mrs Pleshey spoke to Edward Phipps about Rosie's opportunity and he agreed to take Rosie back if it doesn't work out. He expressed his doubts, though, in no uncertain terms.

"She has probably become institutionalized. Don't expect a miracle, Miss Lorrimer, or you will be disappointed."

Mrs Pleshey has given Rosie a tortoiseshell brush and comb that used to belong to her sister. Will Rosie pawn it, I wonder? Maybe, now that she has a washstand and chest of drawers, she will want to display her belongings. I have bought her some underclothes and a simple skirt and blouse, and have given her one of my shawls (the one I no longer like).

Mama has eaten a little – mainly custards and jellies – and dutifully drinks the milk and honey that Amy brings at regular intervals.

Sunday 25th June

Another musical engagement which went well last night, but there was nearly a disaster.

"One of the young men took a fancy to Rosie and gave her a glass of champagne," Theo told me. "It went to her head immediately and she asked for 'more fizz', as bold as brass. I had to refuse on her behalf as I could see she was already getting silly and starting to giggle." He hesitated. "She knows some rather bawdy songs and I was afraid she might decide to sing one."

I laughed aloud but Theo was not amused. "It would have scandalized everyone!"

"I'm sorry." I struggled to keep a straight face. "Did

Rosie give in gracefully?" I asked, already knowing the answer.

It seems she sulked for a few moments but Theo hastily announced the next song and she forgot her bad humour. Poor Theo. His heart must have been in his mouth!

We took Rosie to her little attic room, which was very neat and clean. Curtains fluttered at the window, there was a bright counterpane on the bed and a small rug. A table and chair completed the furniture. Rosie went round touching everything as though to convince herself she wasn't dreaming. We left her with a small picnic for her tea – an apple, bread and cheese. Mrs Defoe promised to keep an eye on her new lodger, and we left Rosie sitting on the edge of the bed, looking very lost.

What will she do? I wondered. She cannot read well enough to enjoy a magazine or a book and she hates to sew. Instead of feeling pleased with myself I returned home with a growing suspicion that we had done the wrong thing.

"Don't be such a ninny!" Theo told me. "We have given her a wonderful chance to change her life."

Tuesday 27th June

Sad news. Mrs Stride has died. They found her dead in bed this morning. The doctor was called in and says he isn't surprised. Her illness was very advanced, she was malnourished and had been severely overworked. So now poor Amos is an orphan. Will he ever be able to find his way alone to his grandparents' cottage? Does he even know the address? Will he have to stay in the workhouse? What a dreadful prospect for the poor lad – his mother and father dead. He is an orphan, but may be too old for an orphanage.

I feel terribly depressed by the news. It seems that poverty goes hand in hand with disaster. We will raise the question of his future at the next meeting.

I didn't tell Mama about poor Mrs Stride – she is still too weak.

But some good news also. Rosie has settled in with Mrs Defoe. So far, so good! I am keeping all my fingers crossed and throwing salt in every direction! Mrs Defoe says Rosie seems rather subdued and goes out a lot. I daresay that after always being with a group of people (in the workhouse), having a room all to yourself is lonely. She has no one to talk to and no one to tell her what to do. She now has to make decisions – when to go shopping, what to spend, what to wear.

I hope Rosie isn't spending time with the awful Jake. Now that she is "a free woman" she is free to make mistakes and Jake could easily lead her astray. I shall suggest she comes here twice a week to continue her writing and reading lessons. I could give her some homework – letters of the alphabet to copy and words to learn. Then there are the times she practises her songs with Theo. Anything to keep her busy and out of mischief.

She really needs a full-time job. I wonder if I have made a mistake by trying to help her to independence too quickly? Still, it is early days. We must wait and see.

Wednesday 28th June

Something truly shocking happened today which left me pale and quaking with fright. A man died not yards from where I stood and I watched it happen. Pray God I may never live through such an experience again. To see a man die is a frightful thing and I shall never forget the horror of it.

I had called in at the workhouse this evening to see how the prayer meeting was being attended. It started at half-past eight but I barely had time to count those present (nine all told) when there was a disturbance in the casual ward. I found Mrs Noye and Mr Phipps facing a bearded man with a broken bottle. He was threatening them and others, and was visibly and hopelessly drunk.

Mrs Noye hissed that it was no place for me to be and I should go. I nodded but did not move. Instead I found myself drawn into the developing drama, little knowing how disastrously it would end.

While Mr Phipps continued to try and reason with him, the other men cowered along the walls, not one of them offering to help us. One man had his fingers in his ears while another, crouched defensively on the floor, had wrapped his blanket round his head. I learned from Mrs Noye that the bearded man's name was John Stratton, one of the men who had caused trouble earlier in the year.

"He's been telling terrible stories about the crimes

he's committed," she told me in a shocked whisper. "Horrible crimes that are sickening to listen to. I don't know whether they are true or not but even the other men are finding them distasteful. If they *are* true, he should have been hanged years ago! He also sang a bawdy song that almost made my hair stand on end. Vile creature. The man's beyond the pale, Miss Lorrimer. Totally corrupt. Try not to listen to him."

We made no move towards Stratton and he seemed too drunk to do more than threaten us. We all waited anxiously as the obnoxious Stratton continued his appalling recital. Fortunately he was so drunk the words were virtually unintelligible – to me at least. Thank the Lord for small mercies, I thought.

When a reedy young constable and a burly sergeant finally entered the room, wooden truncheons at the ready, Stratton erupted into life, roaring defiance, cursing them loudly and threatening to kill them both. As they warily approached him from opposite sides Stratton went berserk and attacked the nearest of them, the young constable, with the broken bottle, narrowly missing his face with the jagged edge. Thankfully, the constable's stout serge tunic bore the worst of the attack. My heart was racing fearfully as I backed away, but as Stratton lunged again the sergeant yelled at him, "Get off my constable, you mad dog! Get back!" and began to clamber forward over the beds. The constable lost his balance and toppled backwards, and Stratton turned and switched his attention to the sergeant. This man, wasting no time in useless argument, immediately swung his heavy wooden truncheon and gave Stratton a blow on the side of the head that knocked him senseless.

As he fell to the floor a loud cheer went up from the other men and Mrs Noye and I exchanged relieved glances. I realized I was trembling.

Phipps cried, "Oh well done, lads!" and without the unholy tirade from Stratton, a kind of peace descended.

The two policemen tried to pull the unconscious man to his feet but his head lolled, his eyes remained firmly closed and his legs refused to support him. They dumped him on one of the beds and leaned over him. The sergeant felt for a pulse, then lifted Stratton's eyelids one after the other. He pursed his lips and then shook his head and my heart began to race with fear as I began to suspect the worst.

One of the casual men called, "Watch the blighter. He's foxy, that one!"

"Not any more!" the sergeant muttered, straightening up and tugging down his tunic. "He's dead."

There was a short, shocked silence. Dead? I was stunned into silence.

Then one of the men muttered, "Good riddance, I say!"

Mrs Noye said quickly, "I second that!"

Edward Phipps strode forward. "We all saw it," he said firmly. "It was self-defence." He looked round the room and there was a chorus of approval for his verdict.

No one expressed a single word of regret and I truly think the world will be a better place without the awful creature, but I feel guilty for thinking so. At least there were plenty of witnesses to swear on the sergeant's behalf.

Thursday 29th June

More trouble. The Board Meeting was cancelled because there were three suspected cases of typhus among the residents. Two elderly men and one woman – all three in the infirmary, separated from the other patients by nothing more than wooden screens. I hope we can avert an outbreak.

I spent some time rereading my diary and still wonder if I could turn it into a book. It is full of intriguing characters. Theo says a story about the workhouse would be too dreary, but people probably said that about the slaves in America and I reminded him that *Uncle Tom's Cabin* is a huge success. Theo had no answer to that, but then declared that at sixteen I am much too young and nobody will take me seriously. But what does he know about writing? He's a musician. (Or thinks he is!)

Sunday 2nd July

Poor Theo. Rosie didn't turn up for their singing engagement and he had to sing alone. At the end of the evening he was paid as a soloist but the people who booked their act were not impressed. I can imagine that much of the sparkle was missing. Rosie had been a very vivacious performer, according to Theo, and very popular. So what happened to her? Theo went round to Mrs Defoe but Rosie wasn't there. Hadn't been there since Friday morning.

"It was her birthday," Mrs Defoe told him angrily. "Or so she said, but who knows whether or not it was the truth! She said no one ever remembered her birthday, but she was seventeen. So I gave her a sixpence by way of a little present and she kissed me and said I was a sweet, kind soul! Then an hour later she was gone and my stuff with her!"

I felt terrible when I heard that, but, birthdays apart, it gets much worse! Mrs Defoe has lost a carriage clock, a barometer and a small gilt snuff box. It looks as though Rosie has stolen them and disappeared. The police were notified and have made some enquiries. Mrs Defoe visited the pawnshops but the items were not there.

I dare not tell Mama – she will be so disappointed. At least here at home the news is better, for Mama is recovering quickly. She came downstairs for an hour this afternoon, which is a real milestone. Cook was so pleased to see her there that she burst into tears of joy and Amy gave Mama a handkerchief she had made for her, embroidered with a single daisy.

I called in at the workhouse this evening to see how

Amos Stride is faring. His face was pale and pinched and I am haunted by his woebegone expression. Enquiries were made into the family, but with no response. Don't the grandparents want the boy? It seems likely he will stay where he is for the next few weeks.

I also enquired after the typhus patients. One of the men has died and been buried. One is recovering. The doctor calls daily and has examined the rest of the residents but found no further victims.

Tuesday 4th July

What a terrible blow! The station master reports seeing a woman like Rosie carrying a cat in a basket. She was with a young man, who had his arm round her, and they seemed very fond of each other. They were waiting for the London train. In my heart I'm sure it was Rosie and Jake and the cat was Oddsey. So they have taken the stolen goods and are off to seek their fortune in London.

Disaster looms and there is nothing I can do about it, but I cannot help feeling partly to blame. We encouraged her to hope for something better and gave her a taste of freedom. Now she has snatched at a chance of a different life, which, with the awful Jake, will almost certainly lead her into bad ways. Even so, for the moment she is probably happier than she has ever been in her life. Should I begrudge her that? At least she has made her own choices – something *we* all take for granted. And could anything be worse than the workhouse? I doubt it.

Theo is angry. He called her an ungrateful wretch, but I know he misses her. And so do I. More than I will admit. Rosie has played a big part in our lives these past months and I had such high hopes for her, but now I fear I will never see her again. What a sad end to her story. I can't help feeling betrayed.

But I refuse to give up trying to help people. I simply won't allow this failure to deter me. Young Amos Stride is in need of help and as soon as Mama is a little stronger I shall talk to her about his future. He will be my new crusade. If we cannot relieve all the misery in the world at least we can do our best for individuals. I have learned much from dealing with Rosie and I won't make the same mistakes again. This time I shall move with more caution.

Friday 15th December

Wonderful, *wonderful* news! A home-made Christmas card has arrived from Rosie Chubb. I had resigned myself to the notion that we would never hear from her again. The card is our first contact since she fled to London in July. It was signed from Bernard, Rosie and Oddsey! A short scrawled message says that Rosie is now singing at a music hall in Stepney where Bernard is a stagehand. So I assume the horrible Jake is no longer part of her life (serving a sentence in Newgate I shouldn't wonder!). Rosie has obviously persevered with her writing lessons. Or maybe Bernard has helped her. Wonders will never cease.

Mama was delighted and has written back to her at the theatre as there was no other address. Mama is almost her old self again, though the doctor warns that she will always be delicate and will find walking difficult. Her life is somewhat restricted now, but at least she can enjoy her comfortable home – a pleasure denied to millions of people.

Theo has been in Milan for months but promises to

return in the New Year. He has been taking singing lessons and hopes to sing "light opera". (Mama is very relieved!)

Young Amos (not so young – he is now twelve) is looking forward to spending Christmas Day with us. The new teacher at the workhouse says he is bright for his age and is already reading sentences from the Bible as well as writing his name and doing simple sums. He comes to us one day a week and we joke that we are "fattening him up"! We sometimes are blessed with a few words from him or a shy smile. Poor lad. Edward Phipps has plans to find him some farm work but we shall try to do better for him. I understand that there is a vacancy for a trainee gardener at Thropston Hall, three miles east of Stoneleigh. Or maybe we can find him a job on the railway. (Either way, he would have a chance of promotion eventually.) We have written to both on his behalf.

Soon 1871 will be over. I have learned so much. Now I wonder, with eager anticipation, what the coming year will bring? This is the last page of my diary and I shall not start another. Instead I think I shall begin my novel…

Historical Note

The British Empire continued to flourish during the 63 years of Queen Victoria's reign. The territories grew in number until Britain ruled a large part of the world. Towards the end of her reign, however, some countries, such as Canada, Australia and New Zealand began agitating for the chance to rule themselves. At the end of the eighteenth century America had already fought, and won, its War of Independence and this process of self-rule continued long into the twentieth century, though as late as the 1930s, primary schools in Britain still celebrated Empire Day with tableaux and processions.

Beneath the glamour of Queen Victoria's reign a huge underclass of her subjects struggled to survive. The main cause for the rapid growth of poverty and civil unrest was the move from the country into the towns provoked by the Industrial Revolution. The continuing change from manpower to mechanical power undermined the labourers who were put out of work and who then flocked to the towns in search of poorly paid jobs in the new factories. And this coincided with an unprecedented growth in the population. Many wealthy people were dismayed by the growing gulf between rich and poor and set up charities, while fair-minded people did their best to raise public awareness by lobbying Parliament. Our modern phrase "Too little, too late" might well have been coined for this situation.

Another serious cause for unrest was the place of women in society. The suffrage movement was born. This demanded the rights of women to a decent education, the chance to earn their own money (and keep control of it) and eventually (in the twentieth century) to be able to vote for a Member of Parliament. Later in her reign the Queen was to offer her support to this cause.

The British Empire was powerful, and by the middle of the century Britain's empire was vast. Trade and commerce expanded rapidly. Towards the end of the century, however, Britain was still adding various territories and millions of people were drawn into the Empire. Because of this, Britain seemed always to be at war somewhere in the world. Mostly, these battles could be considered minor incursions or isolated campaigns, but three events stand out in stark contrast. The Crimean War, the Indian Mutiny, and the Boer War later in Queen Victoria's reign, all of which were major conflicts.

The Crimean War was the conflict that brought the nurse Florence Nightingale to prominence for reorganizing the military hospital at Scutari and improving the conditions of the wounded soldiers there. By revolutionizing medical practices she earned herself a place in history as the "Lady of the Lamp".

There were also, of course, well-documented military defeats that are remembered to this day. Among them are "The Charge of the Light Brigade" (in which cavalry were ordered to ride against artillery at Balaklava, with disastrous results) and the Battle of Isandhlwana during the Zulu wars (when 20,000 Zulus killed 1,200 British troops). Victorian artists were fond of representing such famous events with paint and canvas, and people flocked to the new art galleries to admire their work.

Rural Britain was changing with the advent of steam, and horses would eventually become almost redundant – except for sport. Hunting, shooting and fishing were popular with wealthy landowners and racing was the sport of the ordinary man. (It would take the passionate interest of the Queen's elder son, the Prince of Wales, to make racing fashionable and turn it into the so-called "Sport of Kings".) Boating and cricket were popular, and so were picnics, but the emergence of the bicycle was still some way off.

Travel in Great Britain was transformed by the railways which covered the country, and trains were considered as glamorous as today's aeroplanes. The famous engineer Isambard Kingdom Brunel designed bridges and iron steamships that were to set new standards. Expansion of the railways also gave employment to thousands of Irish labourers known as "navvies".

Abroad, other exciting developments were being undertaken. The Suez Canal was being built (financed by the French); ether had been discovered in America and used as an anaesthetic so that operations could be carried out painlessly for the first time; gold had been discovered in California and Australia, while diamonds *and* gold were found in South Africa.

On the high seas, elegant clippers of American design (large, sleek sailing ships) were bringing tea from China in record time – less than four months! On foreign shores, explorers were mapping remote areas and Dr Livingstone was getting lost in Africa while trying to find the source of the Nile. Eventually he was found in November 1871 by an American journalist. Stanley's casual greeting to him –"Dr Livingstone, I presume?" – has passed into legend.

The Great Exhibition at the Crystal Palace in London in 1851, masterminded by Victoria's beloved husband, was a huge success with the population and was credited with bringing the young queen closer to her subjects. When she died, in 1901, she was mourned by millions at home and abroad.

Timeline

1834 The 1834 Poor Law Amendment Act proposes all the parishes in England and Wales form into Poor Law Unions, each with its own workhouse and supervised by a local Board of Guardians.

1837 Queen Victoria ascends to the throne.

1837 Charles Dickens publishes *Oliver Twist*.

1844 The potato famine begins in Ireland.

1846 The Andover Workhouse scandal. Bone-crushing is abolished in workhouses.

1847 *Jane Eyre*, by Charlotte Brontë, is published.

1851 The Great Exhibition is held at the Crystal Palace. Harriet Beecher Stowe writes *Uncle Tom's Cabin*.

1853 Elizabeth Gaskell publishes *Ruth*.

1853–56 The Crimean War.

1854 Florence Nightingale begins nursing in the Crimea.

1857–58 The Indian Mutiny.

1859 Charles Darwin publishes *On the Origin of Species*.

1860 Charles Dickens publishes *Great Expectations*.

1865 *Alice in Wonderland*, by Lewis Carroll, is published.

1869 The Suez Canal is finished.

John Stuart Mill writes *The Subjection of Women*.
The Charity Organisation Society is founded.
1899–1901 The Boer War.
1901 Queen Victoria dies.

A note on the text
In this book Edith's mother is a member of the Board of Guardians. Although in 1871 women could be Guardians in theory, the first woman wasn't elected to a Board of Guardians until 1875.

Picture acknowledgments

Many new workhouses were built in the nineteenth century. They were usually grim, prison-like buildings.

The casual ward at a workhouse. This is where people were given temporary accommodation.

Dinnertime in the men's section of the workhouse. Men and women were strictly segregated.

An illustration from Charles Dickens's novel, Oliver Twist. *Here Oliver is daring to ask for more food.*

		Breakfast		Dinner				Supper	
		Bread. oz.	Gruel. pints.	Cooked Meat with Vegetables. oz.	Soup. pints.	Bread. oz.	Cheese. oz.	Bread. oz.	Cheese. oz.
Sunday	Men	7	2	5	..	..	..	7	2
	Women	5	2	5	..	..	..	5	1½
Monday	Men	7	2	..	2	7	..	7	2
	Women	5	2	..	2	5	..	5	1½
				Bacon.					
Tuesday	Men	7	2	4	..	..	..	7	2
	Women	5	2	4	..	..	..	3	1½
Wednesday	Men	7	2	..	2	7	..	7	2
	Women	5	2	..	2	5	..	5	1½
Thursday	Men	7	2	..	..	7	2	7	2
	Women	5	2	..	..	5	1½	5	1½
Friday	Men	7	2	4	..	..	..	7	2
	Women	5	2	4	..	..	..	5	1½
Saturday	Men	7	2	..	2	7	..	7	2
	Women	5	2	..	2	5	..	5	1½

A table showing what the inmates at Abingdon Workhouse were given to eat. It must have been a very monotonous and unhealthy diet.

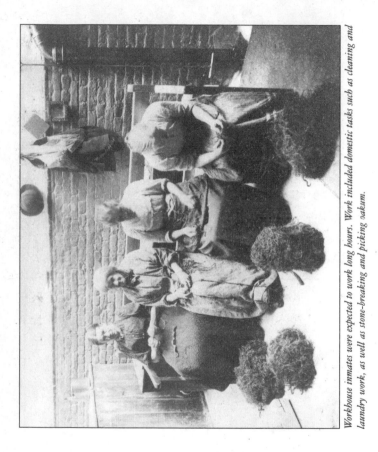

Workhouse inmates were expected to work long hours. Work included domestic tasks such as cleaning and laundry work, as well as stone-breaking and picking oakum.